PRAISE FOR *MIDSUMMER'S MAYHEM*

★ "A delectable treat for food and literary connoisseurs alike."

—*Kirkus Reviews*, STARRED REVIEW

"What a wonderful, intriguing, and magical book. And wow, did it ever get my taste buds going! Each time I picked it up, I felt the urge to head to my kitchen. . . . What I loved most was the smartness of it. It never once doubted its young readers."

—Kathi Appelt, Newbery Honor- and National Book Award-nominated author

"*Midsummer's Mayhem* is an enchantment of a novel bursting with magic, mystery, and mouthwatering baked goods. Readers who have their own baking-show dreams will be cheering for Mimi until the very last page."

—Kate Messner, award-winning author of *Breakout*, *The Seventh Wish*, and *All the Answers*

"*Midsummer's Mayhem* is a delightful confection of a family story full of heart, magic, and a baking championship with mysteriously high stakes! LaRocca takes an almost-throwaway reference in Shakespeare's *A Midsummer Night's Dream* and reclaims it by having a multiracial Indian-American family at the center of her tale. Mimi's pluck, gentle courage, and knack for combining flavors will capture readers' hearts, imaginations, and undoubtedly, taste buds!"

—Sayantani DasGupta, author of the *New York Times*-bestselling Kiranmala and the Kingdom Beyond series

"Taking its inspiration from one of Shakespeare's most popular comedies, *Midsummer's Mayhem* is a sweet and fun story about mistaken identity, bumpy romance, and the everyday magic of baking."

—Barbara Dee, author of *Star-Crossed* and *Halfway Normal*

"Laugh-out-loud funny one moment and mouthwateringly delicious the next, *Midsummer's Mayhem* is an utter pleasure to consume from the very first page! LaRocca's debut novel entices and bewitches—I dare you not to fall under its spell."

—Tara Dairman, author of *The Great Hibernation* and the award-winning All Four Stars series

"Absolutely scrumptious! I fell in love with this book and devoured it in one day. LaRocca crafts a spell of tricky fairies, lovable mortals, and heartfelt magic. Mimi is determined, resourceful, and unfailingly kind. Perfect for aspiring bakers, younger siblings, or anyone with a passion."

—Anna Meriano, author of the Love Sugar Magic series

"Rajani LaRocca has concocted a delectable story about family, friendship, baking, and magic that readers are sure to devour! Relatable, lovable Mimi is easy to root for, and LaRocca brings the whole cast of characters to life with her deft descriptions and realistic dialogue. Readers will delight in *Midsummer's Mayhem*!"

—Erin Dionne, author of *Lights, Camera, Disaster*

"An absolute delight—LaRocca's delectable debut is whimsical, frothy, and so much fun. An inventive take on a classic comedy, *Midsummer's Mayhem* is a sweetly told tale of family, friendship, and following your passion. This is a book for the dreamers and doers alike; effervescent, full of heart, and ultimately joyful."

—Olugbemisola Rhuday-Perkovich, author of *Two Naomis* and *8th Grade Superzero*

"This riff on *A Midsummer Night's Dream* is heartfelt and ridiculously fun. Mimi, sweet as sugar with a heart of gold, creates as many problems as she solves, but readers will be cheering for her and her family the whole way."

—*Booklist*

"An entertaining and epicurean retelling of *A Midsummer Night's Dream* . . . Strikes a perfect balance between the pleasant and the melancholy, as sweet and savory as one of Mimi's confections."

—*Shelf Awareness*

RAJANI LaROCCA

MUCH ADO ABOUT BASEBALL

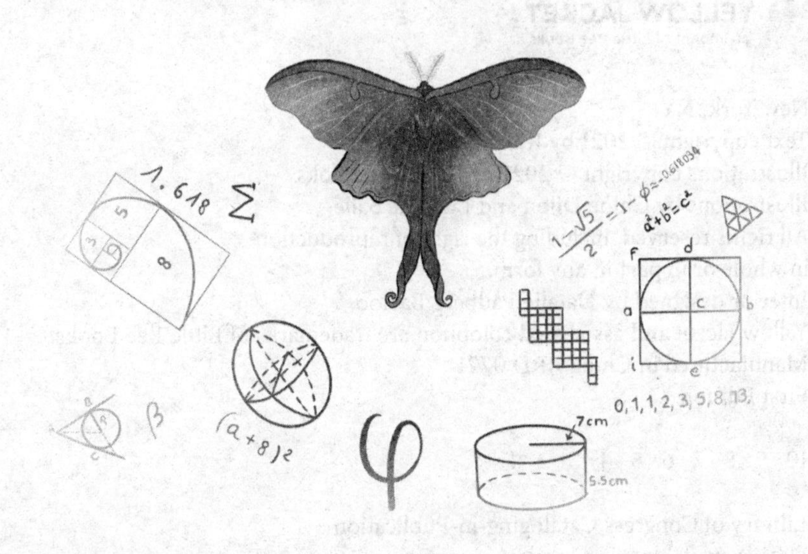

YELLOW JACKET

This is a work of fiction. Any references to historical events, real people, or real places are used fictitiously. Other names, characters, places, and events are products of the author's imagination, and any resemblance to actual events or places or persons, living or dead, is entirely coincidental.

New York, NY

Illustrations by Chloe Dijon and Ludovic Sallé

Interior designed by Natalie Padberg Bartoo

Manufactured in China RRD 0221
First Edition

10 9 8 7 6 5 4 3 2 1

Library of Congress Cataloging-in-Publication
Data is available upon request.
ISBN 978-1-4998-1101-8
yellowjacketreads.com
For information about special discounts on bulk purchases,
please contact Little Bee Books at sales@littlebeebooks.com.

For everyone who's ever wondered

if they belong on the team

Table of Contents

Chapter 1: Baseball Is Magic 1
Chapter 2: The Sign 13
Chapter 3: Prime 27
Chapter 4: Fib's Adventure 36
Chapter 5: The Play 52
Chapter 6: The Thief 58
Chapter 7: Twin Trouble 63
Chapter 8: The Puzzle 80
Chapter 9: The Salt Shaker 92
Chapter 10: The Homer 102
Chapter 11: The Ties That Bind 112
Chapter 12: The Second Puzzle 120
Chapter 13: The Most Important Heart 127
Chapter 14: This Is a Stick 139
Chapter 15: Intense 149
Chapter 16: The Ecstasy and the Agony 159
Chapter 17: Stumped and Slumped 165
Chapter 18: Nowhere Girl 171
Chapter 19: The Last Game 183
Chapter 20: The Golden Ratio 189
Chapter 21: Playoffs and Puzzles 200
Chapter 22: Lost and Found 211
Chapter 23: Sportsmanship 218
Chapter 24: The Championship Game 223

Chapter 25: The Endgame 233
Chapter 26: Hurling 238
Chapter 27: Moths and Magic 242
Chapter 28: Baseball and Broken Hearts 246
Chapter 29: The Final Puzzle 251
Chapter 30: The Ultimate Answer 257
Chapter 31: The Fountain 264
Chapter 32: The Price 272
Chapter 33: The Heart of the Matter 280
Chapter 34: Gifts and Consequences 289
Chapter 35: Forgiveness 294
Chapter 36: Confessions 299
Chapter 37: The Picnic 306

Chapter One

Trish

Baseball Is Magic

Baseball is magic. Time stops between the instant the ball is released and when it makes it over the plate, between the whack of the bat and when the ball finally touches earth again. And this summer, I was holding on to that magic for dear life.

The threads tying me to everything important had snapped, and I was a balloon, floating, flying away on the breeze with nothing to tether me. I was in a new town surrounded by new kids, yanked away from everyone who knew and accepted me.

My brother Sanjay and I were playing catch on a stifling June afternoon in the backyard of our new home. "You'll never be the strongest, so you need to play the smartest," he said as he threw me a scorcher. Sanjay's in high school, and he throws hard, but I got used to hand-stinging catches a long time ago. I'd already run my two miles and finished my push-ups and sit-ups for the day. Physically, I was ready.

"What if no one wants me on the team?" I asked, tossing it back. I'd just left a town where the boys were used to seeing me on a baseball field, but I didn't know what to expect here.

Sanjay caught the ball and laughed. "You're a great teammate, not to mention an amazing ballplayer," he said. "You hit, you run, you deserve a Gold Glove for fielding, and you already throw four-seam and two-seam fastballs. If you can make that circle changeup motion look exactly like your fastball, you'll be a hero." He tossed the ball high in the air, and I moved a few steps to get under it. Sanjay was *my* hero. And he believed in me, no matter what.

The ball smacked into my glove. "I'm just so . . ."

He waited for me to finish, but I didn't want to say the word out loud. *Lost.*

I supposed I could always quit. That might make Mom happy, at least.

"Trish!" Dad called from the garage. "We need to leave now if you want to be early." I tossed the ball back to Sanjay and waved goodbye.

"Ready to meet your new team?" Dad smiled and squeezed my shoulder, but that didn't stop my pulse from pounding in my throat.

"Yeah." I took a deep breath. I had to be the best. That's the only way I'd ever be accepted. So that's what I was going to do this summer.

Mom was at work at the hospital, of course. When she'd landed the chief of cardiology job at Boston General Hospital, it was too good to pass up. Dad could run his graphic design business from anywhere. So we uprooted ourselves from our little town in New Hampshire and moved to Comity, Massachusetts. While Sanjay and I weren't thrilled about changing schools, we didn't have a choice. I knew my brother would be fine. He was so smart, and cute, and hilarious. I was already weird as a girl baseball player and a math kid—well, I *used* to be a math kid—and now I had to make friends with a team full of strangers.

I'd missed travel team tryouts, but I was fine playing in a casual town league. No long trips to games for any of us. And the games were all on weekends, so I hoped that Mom could come to at least a few and not worry about taking too much time off work. Although I knew she'd bring her laptop and would need to keep asking what the score was.

We pulled into the parking lot fifteen minutes before practice was supposed to start.

"Are you sure you don't want me to stay?" Dad asked.

I shook my head. "I'll be fine." I needed to make an impression on my own. "I'll see you in a couple of hours." I smiled in what I hoped was a convincing way as I picked up my bag and climbed out of the car.

I knew it was my last season playing ball. Twelve-year-olds

like me play Little League on a sixty-foot diamond, with forty-six feet between the pitcher's mound and the plate. But in the spring, we move up to the big diamond, which is the size of a Major League infield—ninety feet between bases, and sixty feet six inches from the pitcher's mound to home plate. Lots of boys were already bigger than me. They were growing every second, becoming faster and stronger overnight without even trying. I had serious doubts I'd be able to compete in the spring on the big field. And that was so hard, even harder than moving.

I stopped to survey the baseball fields at Bailey Park. There were two smaller fields and one full-sized diamond where some older players were warming up. The smell of fresh-cut grass and lilacs floated to me. I took a deep breath. There was something in the air. Something that hung like the moment when you take a breath to blow out your birthday candles, and you're not sure what you want to wish for.

I approached the big field where a boy wearing a remarkably sparkly green baseball cap stood at the plate taking practice swings. That hat was incredible. If a baseball cap married a glittery unicorn toy, this would be their baby. As the pitch came in, the boy swung gracefully and was rewarded with the crack of the ball meeting the sweet spot of the bat. The ball sailed over center field, over the fence, and dropped onto the street behind it. If this guy could hit like that—with a wooden bat, no less—he could wear a wizard hat and nobody would care.

An outfielder hopped the fence to retrieve the ball, and everyone else turned back to the boy at the plate, who nodded for another pitch. The pitcher wound up and let go.

Crack. Another perfect swing, and another perfect shot that sailed over left field and bounced off a parked car. It sounded like it left a mammoth dent.

Then the kid switched to a lefty stance and nodded. The pitcher laughed and shook his head, but then wound up and threw again.

This time, the ball sailed over right field and into a dog park, where a golden retriever grabbed it and ran, tail swinging.

How in the world was that boy hitting home runs from both sides of the plate with every single swing? Statistically, that was impossible. If this was the level of talent here in Comity, I was in trouble. I hurried on my way before I lost my nerve completely, and soon arrived at one of the smaller fields, where a coach and a boy were setting up for practice.

"Hello there," said the coach, reaching out and shaking my hand. He was tiny and redheaded, like a slightly oversized elf. "I'm Coach Tom, and this is my son David."

"Nice to meet you, Coach. Hi, David," I said. "I'm Trish."

"Happy to have you on the team this summer," said the coach.

My breathing eased up a little. Apparently, Coach Tom didn't care that I was a girl.

"You two can start warming up while we wait for everyone else," he said.

David, who was already half a foot taller than his dad, nodded and held up a baseball. I ran out onto the field and he started firing throws at me.

After a few minutes, David lobbed a ball way over my head, and it landed on a dead patch and rolled into the woods. I went in after it, and saw a boy there, crouched behind a tree with his eyes squeezed shut. He looked as nervous as I felt.

"Here for practice?" I asked.

The boy opened his eyes and glanced at me, and I couldn't believe it.

I recognized him immediately. Ben. The brilliant math kid who challenged me to do better than ever at the New England Math Puzzler regionals a couple of months ago. He'd been the only sixth grader on his team, just like me. And the best kid on his team, just like me.

I had seen the challenge in Ben's eyes, and I was sure no one could beat him. Neither of our teams won the tournament, but I couldn't believe it when they said I'd gotten the highest individual score. Ben had only missed two points in the final round. But to my surprise, I'd only missed one. Or so I thought.

Standing there in the woods with sunlight filtering

through the trees around us and the birds making a riotous racket, I could tell Ben didn't recognize me. No surprise there, since I'd chopped off all my hair since I last saw him. He was dressed for baseball and carried a sports bag big enough to hold a bat. My mind whirled. I didn't think I'd ever have to face him again. I pulled my cap lower over my eyes.

Ben picked up the ball and tossed it to me underhand. It landed a couple feet in front of me.

"Sorry," Ben said, turning red.

"C'mon," I said, scooping the ball and trotting onto the field.

My mouth went dry when Coach Tom called us all in. We stood in a circle while the coach handed out our uniforms. Ben stood next to another kid, and they put their heads together and whispered and laughed easily. I wondered if I'd ever have a friend like that here in Comity.

"A new local business has donated our jerseys to support the league, so our team name is the Comity Salt Shakers," said Coach Tom. I glanced down at the shirt he handed me: green, blue, and white with a salt shaker logo. Lucky number 7. Too bad I didn't believe in luck. Hard work was the only way to success.

Our team had thirteen eleven- and twelve-year-olds in total. Everyone took turns introducing themselves. Ben's friend was named Abhi. The other players included David and the Mitchell twins, Mike and Garrett. Mike was almost as big as David, with blond hair that reached his shoulders, while Garrett was short, skinny, and dark-haired, with a ratlike nose and a bored expression.

The other two seventh graders on the team were Campbell, a blond kid with braces who never stopped smiling, and Brad, who announced to everyone that he could ride a unicycle, like that had something to do with baseball. There were five tiny soon-to-be sixth graders—this included two boys named Aidan and a freckle-faced kid named George.

And then it was my turn. I swallowed hard. "I'm Trish. I'll be in seventh grade next year."

I looked around, hoping desperately that someone would say something, or smile, or nod. But no one did. Not David, who already knew who I was. Not Ben. He seemed stunned, like a line drive had clocked him in the forehead. Did I look that much like a boy? Or had he finally recognized me from the Math Puzzler tournament?

I crossed my sweaty arms and stared each of them down in turn. "I just moved here from South Ridgefield, New Hampshire. I've been playing ball since I was three. I have three pitches, and I was first in my team's rotation this spring." I'd learned the hard way that you can't show weakness on the field or in the classroom.

Coach Tom smacked his fist into his glove. "Who's ready

to practice? Let's start with grounders. Come with me and I'll explain the first drill." We all followed him onto the field.

By the time practice ended, I'd caught every pop-up that came my way, hit line drives into the outfield, and shown off my two-seamer. When we gathered in the dugout, George the freckle-faced sixth grader tipped his cap at me, the mismatched twins studied me with interest, and Abhi gave me a crooked smirk.

Ben stared at me with his bright blue eyes and I felt exhilarated, like I was back at the Math Puzzler tournament. He'd flubbed some easy catches, though, and most of his throws had been either too short or way too long. I guessed his nerves had gotten the best of him.

As we packed up to leave, Garrett went up to Ben. "Cool shirt."

It was a cool shirt. I'd noticed it right away, and it had made me smile—on the inside, at least. It said, *There are 10 kinds of people: Those who understand binary, and those who don't.*

"Thanks," said Ben.

"Did you bring your calculator?" Garrett asked.

Ben zipped his bag and looked at him. "Why would I—"

"Maybe it'll help you estimate where you need to stand to actually catch something," said Garrett. He and his brother snickered and walked away.

What a jerk!

"*Like the toad; ugly and venomous*," Abhi said to Ben. "Don't worry about him. You're just rusty because you haven't played in a couple years."

Ben shook his head and mumbled something I couldn't hear.

"You'll be fine," Abhi said. "You just need more practice. Come over and we can throw the ball around after dinner."

"I told my mom I'd eat at home tonight. Maybe tomorrow?"

"Sounds good." They bumped fists. Then to my surprise, Abhi turned to me.

"*I can no other answer make but thanks, and thanks; and ever thanks*," Abhi said, bowing like I was royalty. Was he making fun of me?

Ben rolled his eyes. "Is this really the right situation for that quote?"

"Of course. If Trish hadn't won the Math Puzzler Championship this spring, you wouldn't be playing ball this summer. She's a good luck charm already. Right, Trish?" Abhi gave me a grin as my face heated up.

What did that mean?

But before I could ask anything, Abhi took off to the parking lot.

Ben finished packing up. Was he as nervous as I felt? Maybe I could help him. I needed to try. Ben and I both loved math and baseball; I hoped we could be friends.

"Is your glove broken in? Maybe that's the problem," I said.

"I don't have a problem." Ben shoved his batting gloves into his bag. "Just because you're a *star pitcher* and *math champion* doesn't mean you know everything." He hoisted his bag and sprinted to the woods as I spluttered word fragments to his retreating back.

I wondered if he resented having a girl on his baseball team, or if he was still upset about the math tournament. Maybe both?

I plodded to the parking lot to wait for Dad. I needed to find a way to feel good in my skin and on the field and, eventually, in the classroom.

And there was Ben. The boy whose brilliance pushed me to be my best. My math motivator.

He hated me. And he didn't even know all of why he should.

I wasn't going to be able to keep my secret for much longer.

Baseball was magic. And this summer, I needed that magic to work for me.

Chapter Two

Ben

The Sign

Baseball's full of numbers, but that doesn't mean I can play it. I'm good with numbers. They make sense and flip themselves around into patterns in my head so the answer to most problems becomes obvious. Like Mom always says, numbers have sequence and order. Numbers don't lie. Numbers never let you down.

Baseball has stats for everything. It has batting averages, OBPs, and ERAs. But nothing flipped into place when I played baseball. Baseball didn't make sense, at least not to me, not anymore. And baseball let me down. Or, I should say, I let baseball down.

It was the morning of our first game of the summer. I took the last few bites of bagel and reluctantly put down my book on the golden ratio. I'd put baseball off for two years, but now I had to play.

I let my dog Fib lick the last crumbs from my fingers and then bent down to put on my cleats. Fib was a mutt, and to me he was perfect. Ears halfway between floppy and perky, long reddish-brown body turning to gray, and a bushy fox-like tail that never stopped wagging. Fib thumped his tail against the kitchen floor, laid his paw on my leg, and looked at me hopefully.

I scratched him behind his ears and traced the faint white spiral in the soft fur on the top of his head. "We'll bring you, boy, but you need to stay in the shade. It's super hot today." I wished there was something I could give him that would make him able to run like he used to, before his arthritis kicked in. "I'm freaked out, Fib. If only there was some way to magically make me awesome." Fib licked my fingers again and rested his chin on my hand.

Dad walked into the kitchen, and I ducked to retie my shoe.

"Ready to go?" he asked.

I didn't answer right away and started on the second cleat. "Yeah, in a few minutes."

"If we get there early, I'll volunteer to help your coach. I'm going to grab my glove from the shed." Dad slid open the back door and stepped outside.

I frowned and hoped we wouldn't be in time.

Abhi had wanted me to sign up with him for the town's

summer league, "just in case" I wanted to play the next spring. I had no intention of playing in the spring, but Abhi wouldn't let it go. And so we'd made a bet: If I won the Individual Prize at the New England Math Puzzler Championship in April, he wouldn't mention baseball again. But if I didn't win, I'd sign up for summer ball. It was low risk, because I was the best math student in my whole middle school.

But I didn't win. Trish saw to that. I still hadn't gotten over my shock.

I wasn't going to go back on a bet with my best friend. I thought I'd just go to the first practice, then quit. But then Trish showed up. Once I realized she was on the team, I couldn't let her humiliate me again. I was stuck. So here I was, heading straight toward the last thing in the world I wanted to do: play ball.

Trish had messed up the Math Puzzler tournament for me, and now here she was in my own town, ruining everything again.

"Break a bat, Ben," my big sister Claudia said as she breezed into the room.

"What's that supposed to mean?"

"Just trying to wish you good luck, silly," she said, ruffling my hair like I was eight instead of twelve. Claudia's got four years and a good nine inches on me, but still.

"When someone's about to go on stage, you never say good

luck, because that would be *bad* luck," she continued. "So you say the opposite: Break a leg. I tried to think of something similar that was appropriate to baseball."

I rolled my eyes. "You could just say good luck. Not that it will help me. I'm going to be terrible."

"So what?" asked Claudia.

I gaped at her. She *meant* it!

"I mean, isn't that what sports are all about? Bonding with your teammates, having fun, making friends? Why does it always have to be about being the best?"

I sighed. "You don't understand."

Claudia laughed. "You're always so serious, little brother. Lighten up a little. Acting is collaboration, not competition. Maybe you can learn something from me, even though you're the family genius." She curtsied and bowed her head like I was nerd royalty.

"Stop it," I said. I didn't need her mocking me, not today.

"Okay, Ben. Off I go to dress rehearsal," said Claudia. "Only one week until—"

"Opening night. Yes, I know. The whole world knows." Claudia had a major role in the Comity Community Theater production of *A Midsummer Night's Dream*, and it was all she could talk about for weeks. It had something to do with fairies (yuck) and lovers (double yuck) and mysterious happenings in the woods (which did sound somewhat cool, but I wasn't going to tell her that). And she was as excited about this play as I was about solving tricky math puzzles.

"Break a leg," I said.

"Little brother, you do care, after all!" said Claudia. She ruffled my hair again before she sauntered out the door.

For our first game, we were playing one of the two Bridgeton teams—the Bridgeton Cheese Shop Camemberts. The atmosphere became stifling as we drove to Bridgeton, like the other team's hot air was already trying to smother us. I remembered Grandma Beth's advice. *Two, three, five*, I thought to myself. My heart felt as parched and dusty as the infield dirt. I missed her so much.

"Are you excited, Ben?" Dad tried to catch my eye in the rearview mirror. But I wouldn't look at him, and instead concentrated on finishing the bag of sour cream and onion chips in my lap as Fib panted in my ear from his spot next to me.

"I'm so happy to see you play again, Ben," said Mom in a bright voice for the 124th time. "It's a beautiful day for baseball."

"A beautiful day for a massacre," I murmured to myself. Bridgeton always creamed us.

Seven, eleven, thirteen, I thought. I began to feel calmer.

Seventeen, nineteen, twenty-three, twenty-nine.

We pulled up to the field and I grabbed my bag and headed to our dugout. My stomach flipped 3.14 times and resettled itself upside down.

Dad shook hands with Coach Tom. "Good to see you, Tom. I can help out if you need someone."

"I'll take you up on that, Joe," said Coach Tom. "How about third base coach?"

"Sounds good." Dad turned to another dad who'd volunteered. "I'm Joe Messina, Ben's dad."

"Pleasure to meet you, Joe. Deepak Das. I'm first base coach today. That's my daughter Trish warming up out there." I glanced at him. Trish had her dad's big dark eyes.

"Your daughter? That's fantastic," Dad said.

"Trish and Ben already know each other, from April's Math Puzzler Championship. She was from South Ridgefield Middle School in New Hampshire. Trish couldn't stop talking about Ben's amazing performance at the tournament."

Huh? I fished around in my bag and pretended to look for something. I had to hear more of this.

"What?" Dad said in surprise. I hadn't mentioned Trish to him. "She's the other sixth grader, the one who won the top prize? This is amazing—what are the chances that they'd end up on the same baseball team?"

Mr. Das chuckled. "We should ask the kids to calculate that. It's beyond me."

"Me, too. My wife's the math parent in our family. I'm just the baseball guy," said Dad.

I thought for a moment. I couldn't calculate the odds specifically, because there were too many unknown variables: the number of middle school Math Puzzler team kids in the region, the overlap between math and baseball, and the chances that any kid would move from one town to the other. But it was a very, very small chance. It was clearly fate. Unfortunately, it was a bad fate.

Dad was still talking, but I'd heard enough. I jogged onto the field to warm up.

I couldn't help enjoying the sound of kids calling to each other, the sight of balls arcing from hand to glove across a blue summer sky, and the feel of the sun beating on my head. After two years of not playing, it felt like coming home.

Maybe playing ball wouldn't be that bad.

In our league, we played six innings instead of nine, eighteen outs per side instead of twenty-seven. But that didn't mean our games were short. There's no clock in baseball. Time runs differently, and the space between outs can be lightning fast (good if you're the defense) or the span of several lifetimes (good if you're the offense).

As the visitors, we batted first. Their pitcher looked like he needed to shave. How could he possibly be twelve? And the catcher looked like a brick wall who'd somehow been turned into a baseball player.

Trish led off for us, and I knew from practice that she had a fast bat and great running speed. But the gigantic pitcher threw serious heat and had a nasty curve, and Trish could barely get her bat on the ball. She fouled off a few, but eventually struck out looking. Abhi went next and didn't do any better. David batted third and just missed legging it to first base on a decent swing. The top of the first was over in the blink of an eye.

Next it was the Camemberts' turn at bat. The coaches had put me at first base, which shocked me, since it's so important. As a lefty, I had fewer choices in terms of fielding position, but I figured they'd just stick me in the outfield. Had they been talking to Dad? I peeked at him from under my cap, but he was sitting in the dugout waiting for the first pitch. *Thirty-one, thirty-seven, forty-one*, I thought, to chase the nerves away.

Trish was our starting pitcher. She appeared totally calm and composed on the mound, just like she had at the Math Puzzler tournament. She struck out the first two guys like it was nothing. I had to admit she was excellent. Too bad she was such a know-it-all.

I glanced at the stands and saw someone familiar. Sitting next to an old man with long silver hair was none other than the Home Run Kid I'd seen at our first practice. He was still wearing his sparkly psychedelic baseball cap. What was he doing here? Maybe he had a brother on one of the teams?

I had to remind myself to pay attention to the game. The

third batter was another huge guy the size of a grown man, but with a grinning raccoon face. He swung and hit a weak grounder between second and third that was fielded by Abhi at shortstop. He had plenty of time and made an easy throw to me. I was ready. I had a foot on the base, and reached out just like I'd practiced. But the ball hit my glove at an odd angle and bounced off into foul territory. I scrambled to go after it, but the batter had already reached first base. My stomach flipped and flopped irregularly. I'd done this before; I knew disaster was around the corner. My whole team, Dad, Mom, and even Home Run Kid and his dad would get to watch me single-handedly tank the game.

But Trish struck out the cleanup hitter. I'd totally messed up, but she prevented Bridgeton from scoring.

Things went along decently until the third inning, mainly because of Trish's awesome pitching. There were a few hits, but no one scored. We even turned a double play once—Abhi stepped on second base and tossed the ball to me. I didn't have time to think, and the ball miraculously landed in my glove and stayed there.

Back in the dugout, I kept flipping my coin.

"Watcha doing?" asked George. He was my neighbor from two streets over, but we'd never been on a baseball team together. I could feel Trish looking, too.

"It's my lucky coin," I said.

"Cool," George said. He pulled up a pant leg to reveal a gray sock. "I'm wearing my lucky socks. I was wearing them during a game when I stole five bases. Do you have to flip your coin for luck, or is it enough to just hold it?"

"It tells the future. If it turns up more heads than tails, we'll win," I said. "Right now I'm looking at the best of fifty-one."

"You know it's going to turn up close to fifty-fifty heads/tails," Trish interrupted. "That's how probability works."

I looked at her coolly. "This coin predicted the outcome of the last two World Series."

"Although, to be fair, so did most of the country," Abhi said, laughing.

I gawked at him.

Abhi straightened up and put on a serious expression. "But yes, Ben's lucky coin is eerily good at predicting the outcomes of baseball games."

"What does it say now?" Trish asked.

I flipped the coin a final time. "Twenty-seven to twenty-four, tails," I said.

Not a good sign.

We were up to bat again in the top of the third, but the giant Bridgeton pitcher seemed invincible. Our first batter, one of the Aidans, struck out on three pitches. I took a few nervous practice swings on deck as George got up to the plate. He bunted a perfectly placed ball and rabbited to first base.

Now it was my turn to bat. *Forty-three, forty-seven, fifty-three.* I took a breath and stepped into the batter's box.

It was like I entered another dimension. All I could see was the pitcher's Neanderthal glare under his unibrow. With something that scary in front of me, how could I possibly pay attention to the ball? One second, it was in his meaty paw, and the next second, it slammed into the catcher's mitt. I kept missing the part where I had a chance to swing. After two strikes looking, I was desperate to make contact. On the third pitch I swung wildly and the bat connected. I sprinted to first base only to be confused when I found George still there. "Foul ball," he said. "Go back."

I jogged back to home plate and tried to psych myself up. *I can do this. Fifty-nine, sixty-one, sixty-seven.* Trish was taking warm-up swings like she might actually get to bat after me. Was Home Run Kid still in the stands? I cringed thinking of a guy with that much talent watching me fail at the plate.

The next pitch was a ball up near my helmet, and I didn't swing. One ball, two strikes. One more pitch hurtled toward me, and I threw my hands out and connected again. It was a weak ground ball. The shortstop grabbed it, stepped on second base, and tossed it to first. A double play. I had blown our chance to score. I glanced over at Dad standing near third base. He shrugged and frowned.

I kicked the dirt. I'd ruined our chances with a single

swing. I walked back to the dugout in a daze.

"Good try," Trish said as she followed me.

"You don't have to rub it in." I scowled at her and stalked away.

And then came the bottom of the third. Trish was pitching to the meat of their order. She got two strikes on Brick Wall with her first two pitches, and on the third swing the batter popped one up between the pitcher's mound and the first base line. It was my ball. I scanned the sky. *Seventy-one, seventy-three, seventy-nine.* There it was! Nothing existed but the ball—I shut out the brightness of the sun, the sweat dripping into my eyes, and the murmur of the people in the stands. I kept my eye on the ball and scurried to where I thought it would come down. *Eighty-three, eighty-nine, ninety-seven, one hundred one.*

In the sky, a flock of black birds formed a spiral, then moved in a feathered wave, flying off like they'd all received the same instructions. I stopped focusing on the ball for a split second. It was a sign! But of what? Was luck on our side or not?

My head collided with what felt like a block of cement. I tripped and fell, stepping on something soft.

Suddenly, the sound in my world got switched back on. "Get *off*!" I heard as someone shoved me. A pair of feet thundered past me. I found myself lying in a heap on top of Trish and scrambled to get off her. Apparently, she had been trying to catch the ball, too. Dimly, I saw David, the catcher, grab the ball that had rolled from underneath us, but not until the runner had already reached second base.

I hurried to stand, but Trish stayed on the ground. She held her wrist and peered up at me, grimacing and squinting into the sun. "Why'd you keep going after that ball? Didn't you hear me call it?"

I shook my head numbly. I had been paying attention to nothing but the ball, just like everyone had always told me. Okay, the birds had distracted me, but that was for just a second.

Coach Tom called time and came over, and the rest of the team converged.

Trish's dad held her wrist to examine it, and she winced when he pressed on the outer part. He moved it around gently, and she gritted her teeth. "How's your head?" he asked.

"Fine," she said with a grimace.

"I don't think your wrist's broken, but it might be a nasty sprain. We should wrap it up and ice it right away. We'll get it x-rayed after the game."

"But Dad—"

"I agree," said Coach Tom.

"Okay." Trish closed her eyes again.

Trish's dad turned to me. "You okay? Anything hurt?"

I shook my head. I was fine. I had just incapacitated our best player, but there wasn't a scratch on me.

The coin had been right.

Trish's dad helped her up, and she walked to the dugout holding her wrist as everyone in the stands applauded her.

Coach Tom called the team in. "Okay, guys, keep your head in the game. Mike, you're in to pitch," he said. "Start warming up." Mike nodded and went to the mound.

When I got back to first base, Brick Wall gave me a gigantic grin and a thumbs-up from his spot on second base.

He was right. I was the biggest gift our opponents could hope for.

That was the end of any chance we had of beating the Bridgeton Camemberts. They scored five runs that inning alone. They ran around the bases, chanting, "CHEESE ALWAYS WINS! CHEESE ALWAYS WINS!"

Even worse, their coach kept telling them to steal bases and run up the score. It turned out that the players weren't the only goons on that team.

The final score: 11–1 Bridgeton. Another baseball game I managed to destroy single-handedly.

Baseball was a team sport, but it only took one Ben to lose.

Chapter Three

Trish Prime

"But it's Sunday morning," I said to Mom. Sunlight streamed through the large window in the kitchen and lit up her face. Her eyes were puffy and her mouth sagged. "You didn't come to our first game. Why can't you come to this one?"

Mom slid her laptop into her bag and hoisted it onto her shoulder. "I'm sorry, Trisha." Her voice was scratchy. "I've got cell cultures in the lab that need tending, or they'll be ruined."

I crossed my arms. "Can't someone else do that today?"

"We've already discussed this," said Mom. "There is no one else right now. But I'm hiring someone as soon as I can. And you're not even playing today, not with that wrist."

I sighed. Mom is a heart doctor, not a wrist doctor, but she's still the medical authority in our home. But it didn't matter that I wasn't playing. I wanted her to see me on my new team.

I wanted her to see me.

"I know you're disappointed. But you know what it's like to do important work," Mom said. "You've sacrificed so many hours for math. You're always prepared, you work hard, and you never take shortcuts. But it's worth it to shine like you do."

I bit the inside of my cheek and ran my hand over the newly shortened hair at the nape of my neck. How could I ever tell her that I hadn't actually won the Math Puzzler tournament? And what would she say when I told her I wasn't going to try out for the Math Puzzler team this year?

"In any case, I'm glad your baseball career will be over soon. I know it's been fun, but we can't risk you getting injured again. It could have been a concussion. Or worse."

"I'm fine. Baseball's usually a low-contact sport," I grumbled.

"I'll be happy when the fall comes and you can concentrate on academics again. If you want more exercise, maybe you could take up dance?"

"I'm not going to take up dance. Like it's that easy to start that when you're twelve."

"You can do anything." She kissed me on the forehead, squeezed me in a hug, and walked away.

If she knew the truth about the Math Puzzler tournament, would she still think that?

But when could I tell her? Ever since my parents decided to move, Mom was so busy—tying up her old practice, packing, and now that we were here, she was too busy at the hospital and in the lab to even unpack all her stuff at home. Half her clothes were still in boxes. I offered to help, but she always had to do everything herself.

"Even when you hire someone, you'll still find a reason to go in," I whispered to no one.

We arrived at our field at Bailey Park to play our second game on an oppressively hot morning. We were playing a team called MacAllister's Sporting Good Guys from another nearby town, Banbury. I settled myself on the bench and prepared to score the game.

Numbers are important in baseball. They give us a system to keep track of what's happened. Each fielding position has a number assigned: 1 and 2 for the pitcher and catcher; 3, 4, 5 for first, second, and third basemen; 6 for the shortstop; and 7, 8, and 9 for left, center, and right field. A code for the scorebook, so we can analyze what happens in each game and figure out how to plan our batting order and pitching rotation.

Even if I couldn't play, at least I could help my team this way. Information was crucial.

My fingers itched as I watched Abhi pitch. Although my wrist was only sprained, it still ached, even taped up. We only had nine more games before the playoffs, and the last thing I wanted was to sit on the bench for any of them. They were all that was left of my baseball career. But it couldn't be helped. I sighed and recorded the other team's final out of the second inning (groundout, 6–3) in the scorebook.

Ben sat near me on the bench, but he acted like he didn't know I was there as he finished a bag of salt and vinegar potato chips and kept score in his own notebook. I wasn't sure how he was doing it, though, since he barely watched the game. He was like a problem that had no solution, like dividing by zero. I knew he didn't like me, but it surprised me that he hadn't even apologized for knocking me over and stepping on my throwing wrist.

Abhi pitched two scoreless innings. We were ahead 1–0 and up to bat again at the bottom of the second.

I smiled at Abhi as he sank onto the bench. "Great start," I said.

Ben gave him a fist bump. "Awesome start," he said.

"Trish, you threw amazingly yesterday. Could you give me some pitching pointers when your wrist is better?" Abhi asked.

I glanced at Ben. I didn't want to sound like I was showing off. "Coach is going to work with the pitchers at practice on Tuesday."

"That is, if you can even practice with that wrist injury," came a voice. Garrett stood over Ben. "Too bad Benny wasn't the one who got hurt. Benny doesn't pitch." Garrett's beady little eyes glittered. "Or bat, or catch. He's worse than a girl."

Ben turned bright pink. My face heated up, too.

"Dude, we're all on the same team," Abhi said. "And Trish

played awesome yesterday before she got hurt. And she's a girl."

"No offense," Garrett said with a simper. "But you can't pitch with your wrist like that."

"I'll be okay in a couple days," I said. I tried to move my wrist but couldn't help wincing at the pain. "Besides, we should root for each other."

"I don't see Benny rooting for us," said Garrett. "He's barely paying attention. What're you doing, Benny? Calculating how lame you are?" He snatched Ben's notebook, glanced at the open page, and tossed it in my lap with a laugh. "See? He's not keeping score. He's just writing out a bunch of stupid math problems."

I frowned and glanced at Ben's notebook. Garrett was right. I squinted at Ben's scrawl; some of the problems seemed interesting.

"Give that back!" Ben snatched the notebook and glared at me like I was the one who had taken it. Garrett continued to snicker.

"Guys, stop talking and pay attention to the game," Coach Tom snapped.

Abhi nodded at the field. "Garrett, you're on deck," he said.

Garrett gave Ben a dirty look, picked up his bat and helmet, and strutted onto the field. Ben slumped on the bench.

Abhi turned his head back and forth at Ben and me from his spot between us as the batter grounded out. "How about those Turkeys?" he whispered.

I figured Abhi was trying to distract us from Garrett, but I didn't believe it would work on Ben so easily. Ben smiled, and he looked like a completely different kid from the sullen one a moment earlier. "That was a great series against New York," he said. The New England Turkeys, our Major League team, currently had the best record in baseball.

"You can say that again," I said. At least there was something we could agree on.

"They are amazing," Abhi said. "And our team's going to be amazing, too."

I turned back to the game. Garrett smacked a single—that kid was a good ballplayer, even if he was a jerk—and now Mike was at bat with two outs. *1B*, I wrote.

Ben flipped his coin and looked at his hand. "Five heads, four tails. We might have a chance today."

I couldn't help rolling my eyes.

"The coin knows," Ben said. He almost smiled before he put his guard up again and turned away.

I looked down as something wet touched my hand. A black-nosed, brown-haired dog was wagging his entire body and licking my hand like it was made of bacon.

"Hi there, sweet doggy," I said. "Where'd you come from?"

"Fib!" Ben barked. "You're not allowed in the dugout. Get out of here!"

"Oh, let him stay for just a bit. He's such a good boy," I said. "And did you say his name is Fib? Is that short for—"

"He's not allowed in here. I'm taking him back to the stands. Claudia's supposed to be watching him. Come on, Fib. Now." Ben grabbed the dog's collar and led him away.

Campbell drew a walk to load the bases. Brad stepped up to the plate, and Abhi stood. "I'm on deck," he said. "Don't worry about Ben. He's great once you get to know him." He smiled tentatively.

"I'm sure," I said as Abhi took his bat and walked to the field.

Well, someone with a dog that sweet couldn't be all that bad.

But Ben was still scowling when he returned to the dugout.

"Eighty-three, eighty-nine, ninety-seven, one hundred one," I whispered.

"What?" Ben drew back, his eyes wide.

"I heard you say that yesterday. Right before we crashed."

He glowered at me. "So?"

"So, I know what they are."

Ben narrowed his eyes. "Yeah? What's next?"

"103, 107, 109, 133. Primes." Numbers that are only divisible by one and themselves. They're unusual, special, unique. Like Ben. Like me. Math kids and baseball lovers.

"Right." He let out a breath. "They . . . uh . . . help me concentrate. I didn't realize I was saying them out loud. So fine. I'm weird."

I shrugged. I didn't think that was weird. "What's with all

the primes in that last problem you wrote?"

Ben looked up and studied Brad fouling off a pitch, but his cheeks had turned pink again.

"Seriously. Can I take a look?"

He smirked and handed me his notebook. "Go ahead," he said. "It can be like practice for Math Puzzler team tryouts." He smiled at me like a cartoon villain, and my heart sank. He wouldn't want me on the team if he knew my secret.

But if I wasn't going to be on the team, it was going to be because *I* chose not to. Not because Ben told me I couldn't.

I lifted my chin. "Then I'll give you one so you can practice for next year's Math Puzzler Championship."

That wiped the grin off his face.

The problem read: *I am a whole number under 100. When counted in threes, 2 are left over, when counted in fives, 3 are left over, and when counted in sevens, 2 are left over. What am I?* My mind whirred as Brad fouled off yet another pitch and Abhi took a couple more practice swings.

"Well? Need some help?" Ben asked.

As if! "Hold on a sec, let me think." Three left over after counting in fives. That means it ends in a three or an eight. But what about the other two clues? Okay, two are left over with *both* threes and sevens. That was the key!

I could feel Ben turn his face toward me. He had a kind of heat to him, like the sun. I forced myself to look at him.

"Twenty-three," I said.

"You got it. Not bad," he said. But he appeared disappointed.

"Now here's one for you." I scribbled on a blank page in the back of my notebook, ripped it out, and handed it to him. It read:

1 11 21 1211 111221 312211

"What comes next?" I asked Ben.

He glanced at the paper and frowned.

Brad struck out.

"Listen up!" called Coach Tom. He looked at his chart. "Aidan P, you're in at second base. Ben, you're in right field."

Ben stood, still scrutinizing the piece of paper with my puzzle on it.

"Hold on to it," I said. "I can help you if you can't solve it on your own."

Ben scowled at me as he folded the page and shoved it in his pocket. Then he ran out to right field.

Ben wasn't going to be able to solve that problem. It was going to drive him batty, and I was going to enjoy watching him squirm.

Because it wasn't a math problem.

Chapter Four

Ben

Fib's Adventure

I stood in right field thinking about that swirl the birds had made in the sky the day before. It was clearly a sign for our team. For me. But what did it mean?

My mind drifted to Trish. She knew her math, all right. She'd solved my problem in five seconds flat. But she was so infuriating! That was a low blow, mentioning the Math Puzzler Championship and rubbing it in like that. And what was up with her problem? I couldn't figure out any way to connect those numbers. They kept spinning in my head, but they weren't flipping into any type of pattern. The numbers taunted me.

"Ben! Heads up!" Coach Tom's voice snapped me out of my math puzzling. I looked up just in time to see a baseball hurtling toward me from the sky. I could hear Garrett's mocking voice in my head.

The ball dropped right next to me, and by the time I'd scrambled to pick it up and throw it back to the infield, the runner had advanced to second base. He went on to score their first run.

Abhi held the other team to two runs, but had to come out because he was pitching for his travel team in a couple days. The Sporting Good Guys scored two more runs off David in the sixth, and we ended up losing the game 4–1.

Abhi sat next to me in the dugout as the coaches debriefed us.

"The coin called it again," I said, shaking my head. "I tried for best of one hundred and one, but it ended up tails, fifty-two to forty-nine."

But Abhi grinned; it didn't seem to bother him that we might not win a single game the whole summer. "So . . . Trish. She's pretty cool, right?"

I rolled my eyes. "She's excruciating. I can't believe we have to deal with her."

Abhi's face fell.

"Boys, pay attention," said Coach Tom. Trish readjusted her cap and smirked at us from her seat next to him. "Great game," Coach said. "We may not have won, but we had great pitching, great hitting, great teamwork. We're all in it together, and when everyone's head's in the game, we all benefit."

Everyone nodded like they actually believed it.

"Make sure you pick up all your stuff. We'll see you Tuesday afternoon for practice."

I packed my bag and trudged to the stands to Mom and Dad, hoping to get another glance of Home Run Kid. But although he'd watched for almost the whole game with Silver-Haired Man, now he was nowhere in sight.

"Good game, Ben," said Dad. I knew he'd been itching to be third base coach again, but luckily one of the other dads had beaten him to it.

"Well, I didn't get a hit or catch anything, but at least I didn't incapacitate a teammate this time," I said.

He furrowed his brow. "That should have been a hit for you, in the fifth."

Yeah, if I'd worked harder, practiced more, turned my hips . . . all of Dad's advice echoed in my head. I sighed. I didn't belong on this team, but I couldn't quit, thanks to my stupid bet and annoying Trish.

Claudia had come with us, but she was sitting in a different part of the stands from my parents, deep in conversation with some guy. Of course. That's why Claudia had stayed for the whole game—I knew she had absolutely no interest in my baseball career.

"Where's Fib?" I asked Claudia. It annoyed me that she'd let him wander over to the dugout during the game. What if he'd gotten clocked by a foul ball? He was old and might not be able to get out of the way fast enough.

She glanced around. "He must be in the woods. He was sniffing around at the edge of the field a little while ago. Can you go get him?"

"You were supposed to be watching him. Why don't you go get him?"

"I'm busy right now," Claudia said, smiling at the guy.

"Sanjay," said the guy with a nod at me. "I'm Trish's—"

"Hey Sanjay, Dad said we're going to pick up lunch on the way home. What do you want?" came a voice next to me. Trish glanced at me, then took a step back in surprise.

"And here's Trish," Sanjay said.

Claudia smiled her biggest smile. "Hi, Trish. I'm Claudia, Ben's sister. Our dog Fib wandered into the woods. Want to go look for him with Ben?"

I glowered, hoping Trish would take the hint, and waited for her to say she was tired, or too busy, or didn't like the woods. I didn't think she'd say she hated my guts. At least not out loud. I gritted my teeth as I remembered her smug look, the way her eyes bored into mine in triumph, when she was announced the Individual Prize winner at the Math Puzzler Championship in April.

"Sure," said Trish. "Fib's a sweetie."

Wait. What?

Fine. I dropped my bag at Claudia's feet, grabbed Fib's

leash, and stalked to the woods. Trish could follow along if she wanted but we weren't going to be in there for long. Fib couldn't have gotten far; he could barely make it half a mile nowadays because of the pain in his legs. He limped so much sometimes that it hurt to watch. But he was always wagging and ready to go out. And he loved the woods. He sniffed at little critters that lived in the brush and waded into the stinky creek that flowed into the Sketaquid River. And when he swam, Fib almost looked like a young dog again.

I stepped into the woods and looked around. The trees were sparse at the edge of the field, but I couldn't see Fib anywhere.

"Fib," I called. "Here, boy!"

No dog appeared.

"Does he usually come when he's called?" asked Trish.

"Yep," I said as calmly as I could. Of course my dog was trained. "He can't be far. Fib," I said. "Come!"

Still no dog. I was irritated, hot, and tired. And I didn't want to spend a minute more with Trish than I needed to.

We followed the path farther in where the trees were closer together. This was the way home. Maybe Fib headed that way by instinct? The leaves barely stirred in the muggy air as we walked slowly down the path, scanning for Fib. I could smell warm earth and a slight tang of swampy water.

I thought I knew the Comity Woods. Pine needles crunched

under our feet, leafy trees split the sunlight into unfathomable patterns, and birds chirped mysterious communications as we trotted on the path that led from Bailey Park toward my house. But the path didn't seem straight anymore. It took jogs to the right, and turns to the left, and we passed two droopy evergreens leaning on each other like old men, trees I was sure I'd never seen before.

Then I spotted a guy walking toward us. I recognized him. It was Home Run Kid!

He looked like he was about sixteen. He wasn't huge, but he was definitely athletic. Blond hair stuck out from under his sparkly baseball cap.

"What have we here," he said. "Two friends in the woods, and it's nearly midsummer."

I stood there with my mouth hanging open. I had no idea what he was talking about, but it was like meeting a celebrity!

"Have you seen a dog run through here? He's brownish-red with a bushy tail," Trish said.

"Sorry, I haven't. I do hope you find him, though. It's quite distressing to lose a companion." Home Run Kid had a funny accent, and I couldn't tell if he was from another area of the country or another country altogether.

"We've seen you at Bailey crushing home runs," I blurted. Maybe if I hung out with this kid, some of his baseball magic would rub off on me? I could use all the help I could get.

Home Run Kid grinned, but then smiled sadly. "I love smacking the ball around with the guys. I adore baseball. And soccer, football, rugby, lacrosse, basketball." He counted off on his fingers. "Rounders, curling, hockey, badminton. Sailing, pole vaulting . . . I play pretty much everything. Alas, though, no more ball games for me this summer." He took his cap off, revealing a head full of blond curls, then put it on again backward.

"How come?" Trish said.

"Summer obligations," the kid said.

"I know what that feels like," I said. Only my obligation was to play, instead of not to play. I looked around. Where the heck was Fib? "We'd better get going," I said half-heartedly.

"Hang on," the kid said. He stuck out his hand. "I'm Rob. Lovely to meet you both."

Lovely? I eyed his hand. Grown-ups usually shook hands. We shook. "Ben. And my dog's name is Fib, if you see him."

"That's a strange name," said Rob.

"It's short for Fibonacci," I said.

"He was a famous mathematician," Trish added. Such a know-it-all. Why was she explaining *my* dog's name?

"Ah. So in addition to being baseball players, you both know a lot about mathematics?" Rob leaned toward us both, like he couldn't wait to hear our answer.

"Kind of," Trish and I said in unison. Annoyed, I glanced

at her, but she seemed serious. Thanks to her, I was no longer the best kid mathematician in town, or even in the upcoming seventh grade class.

Rob tilted his head. "Fascinating. What did Fibonacci do that made you name your dog after him?"

"My mom did the naming—she's a math professor," I said. "She named him because of a spiral mark in his fur. Fibonacci the mathematician lived in the 1200s and described an interesting sequence of numbers where each number is the sum of the two before it."

Rob looked blank, like I had suddenly started speaking a different language. I was used to this.

Trish piped up again: "The sequence is: 0, 1, 1, 2, 3, 5, 8, 13, 21, and so on."

"But why is that interesting?" Rob tilted his head again.

"Well for one thing," I said, searching on the forest floor around me, "it's found over and over again in nature." I grabbed a pine cone and held it up. "See? If you count the diagonals, there are eight going one way, and thirteen going the other way. Those are both Fibonacci numbers." I handed the pine cone to Rob, who took it from me with a stunned expression.

But Trish wouldn't let up. "And there are lots of other Fibonacci numbers in the natural world. I don't know much about flowers, but I've read that many have numbers of petals that are Fibonacci numbers."

Rob squinted at the ground between us. "What are the numbers? For the petals?"

"Uh, three . . ." I said.

"Lily. A lily has three petals," said Rob.

"Five . . ." Trish said.

"Buttercup."

I hurried to say the next one. "Eight . . ."

"Delphinium." Wow! This kid knew flowers *and* baseball.

"Thirteen, twenty-one . . ." Of course Trish had to name the next *two*.

"Marigold, and black-eyed Susan." Rob looked at us, and his eyes seemed to light up. "And is there a thirty-four? And a fifty-five?"

"Yeah," I said, surprised. "And then—"

"Eighty-nine!" Trish and I spoke at the same time.

"Sunflowers," Rob said, laughing.

It wasn't funny. It was like being in the tournament all over again. Why was this girl always showing me up?

"Wow. You know a lot about flowers," Trish said.

"Among other things." Rob winked.

I raised my voice to drown out whatever Trish was going to say next. "If you use the Fibonacci numbers to make squares, and trace a line from corner to corner, you make a spiral that's also found everywhere in nature, from snails to hurricanes. And that's what the spiral on Fib's forehead reminded Mom of."

Rob smiled warmly at us. "Both of you have such marvelous mathematical minds, and you're on the same baseball team. It must be wonderful to spend the summer together."

For once, Trish said nothing. I joined her in silence but peeked at her out of the side of my eye.

"Come now, you two. You must be friends," said Rob.

I stared at the ground, but I could feel Trish looking at me.

"Our team's not doing very well," I said.

"You know, perhaps I could help you with that," said Rob.

"With baseball? You mean, like give me—I mean, us—pointers?" My heart sped up and my stomach contracted.

"In a way." Rob looked at me, and my insides went all squirmy. His eyes seemed brighter than normal. But that was ridiculous. "The first tip is: Always keep your eye on the ball."

Trish furrowed her brow. "Everyone knows that."

"Ah, but have you heard of this? Talk to the ball, tell it what to do."

I frowned. "What's that supposed to mean?"

"Exactly what I said."

"You're messing with us," I said.

Rob laughed and turned his sparkly baseball cap the right way around again. "No, no, I'm not. I mean it. Sports is almost all mental. Teamwork is essential. And so is food."

"You mean, like no junk food?" Trish asked.

"I'm not giving up chips for anything," I said.

"No need to," said Rob with a grin. "I have these nutritious snacks. Tasty, but full of vitamins that really boost sports performance." He flexed a bicep that, I had to admit, was impressive.

"Like energy drinks?" Trish asked.

"Somewhat, but so much more delicious. Now I will not say they are miraculous—but they certainly help with sports performance. They're all made as part of my family business. You should visit the Salt Shaker sometime. We have loads of great snacks there, for athletes and intellectuals alike."

I looked at him blankly. What did Comity's new snack shop have to do with anything? Was this why they were sponsoring our baseball team?

Trish narrowed her eyes at Rob. "They're not . . . performance enhancing, right? Like, that's unethical. And illegal."

Yikes! Rob couldn't possibly mean that, could he?

Rob laughed. "No no no, nothing like that. Unlike others we know, *we* play according to the rules at the Salt Shaker."

Trish seemed relieved. "My mom doesn't like me eating fried food. But I suppose we should go there, since we're the Salt Shaker's team." She turned around to show Rob the back of her jersey.

Rob snapped his fingers. "Of course! Yes, you must come

by the Salt Shaker some time. Some of our selections can help with teamwork."

I rolled my eyes. How could food do that? And the last thing I needed was more *teamwork* with Trish.

"What about a baseball clinic, or something? I bet lots of kids would love to learn from you," I said.

Something rustled in the brush behind me. I turned to look, but there was nothing there.

When I turned back around, Rob was gone.

As in, completely. "Where'd he go?" I asked.

Trish shook her head. "I have no idea. He was standing right there, but I turned around to see what made that noise, and then he was gone."

We looked around nearby and behind several trees, but it was like Rob had evaporated.

From the brush behind us came a yip, the one Fib made when he encountered a doggy friend he wanted to play with. He couldn't be hurt, because that definitely sounded like a happy bark. Or was it? A pang of guilt gnawed at me. I shouldn't have spent so much time with Rob.

Fib emerged from the bushes and barked his puppy bark again. I could tell by the spark in his eyes and his furiously wagging tail that he wanted to play.

A wave of relief washed over me. "Fib, you doofus. What're you doing all the way out here? The game's over. Let's go home."

Fib completely ignored me, ran to Trish, jumped all over her, and kissed her madly.

"Oh, Fib, what a good boy!" Trish giggled as Fib licked her taped-up wrist.

What had gotten into him? I grabbed his collar and looked him over. He seemed fine—no obvious injury. Then I looked more closely at his face as he smiled his doggy smile. "What have you been eating?"

Fib's muzzle was wet and covered in green dust. He licked a smudge off his nose like he understood what I was saying.

"No treats from Mom if she finds out you've been eating deer poop," I said as I clipped the leash on his collar. "Did he get that stuff on you?" I asked Trish.

"Yeah, but it's okay," said Trish, wiping her hand on her baseball pants and leaving a green smear that matched the grass stains already there.

"Come on, let's get back," I said.

I had to practically drag Fib out of the woods—whatever he had found in there, he was in love.

We headed back on the path and when we finally got to the edge of the field, I broke into a jog. I really wanted to get home. The stands had cleared out except for Claudia and Sanjay.

"Took you long enough," said Claudia, raising one eyebrow dramatically and lifting her hair off the back of her neck. "We've been waiting for ages."

"Maybe you should have kept a better eye on Fib during the game," I shot back.

"Sorry. That's my fault for distracting her," said Sanjay. "We should get going. But we'll see you next Saturday for sure. Claudia's just invited us to come see her in *A Midsummer Night's Dream* next weekend."

What?

Trish appeared to be as horrified as me, at least.

"We should go. I'm starving," I said to Claudia, who reluctantly tore her eyes away from Sanjay and followed me.

"See you next week," she said to him. "I'll save good seats for you and Trish."

I started jogging toward the parking lot. "Hurry up," I said.

Mom and Dad were already at the car putting away my stuff. Mom gasped as we reached her.

"Ben!" she said. "What happened to Fib?"

"What do you mean?" I glanced over, and Fib seemed okay—his tongue was lolling out of his mouth, but it was ninety degrees outside.

"Fib, come," said Mom. I let go of the leash, and Fib scampered up to her and put his paws on her legs.

"See? He's fine," I said.

"Fine? Ben, he just ran across the field with you. Ran! And now look at him!"

I looked. Fib licked Mom's hand and then trotted over to

me. He scooted his butt into the air and pushed his front paws out straight. A play bow. I hadn't seen him do that in forever, not since the arthritis had gotten really bad. He frisked around me and chased his tail like he was five years younger. My sweet old dog seemed to have aged backward in the space of a baseball game.

"It's like he went into the woods and found the Fountain of Youth," Mom said.

Now what were the odds of that?

Chapter Five

Trish

The Play

My dad and Ben's were now the official assistant coaches. This seemed to make Ben unhappy, although I couldn't understand why. Mr. Messina was a good coach and encouraged all the players on the team, including Ben, but Ben looked like he was constantly trying to escape his dad's attention.

The next Saturday morning, we lost our third game 4–2 to another Comity team, Margherita's Pizza Players. I was back playing, although Dad wouldn't let me pitch. The whole team acted sluggish and cranky. Ben hadn't said a word to me after our weird little adventure in the woods, and I could guess why: He still hadn't solved the puzzle I'd given him.

"Maybe you should go on your own to Claudia's play tonight," I told Sanjay over dinner. "I don't feel like it." Mom was at the hospital again, of course, so it was just the three of us.

"She invited both of us," he said. "Besides, it'll help cheer you up after today's game. It's a funny play about magical happenings in the woods. And you'll get to spend more time with your baseball buddy and fellow super math nerd, Ben."

My shoulders sagged. I appealed to Dad. "Won't you be lonely at home all alone?"

"I'm looking forward to watching the last *Rock 'em and Sock It* movie in the living room tonight," Dad said. "You're welcome to join me."

Given the choice between endless car chase scenes and Shakespeare, I chose Shakespeare. "I guess I'll come to the play after all."

"Great. It'll be fun, I promise," Sanjay said.

I wasn't so sure.

Claudia couldn't have asked for a more perfect evening. The play was being performed on an outdoor stage that backed up to the woods. The setting certainly looked magical, with clear skies, a slight breeze, and the sun hanging low in the sky like a fiery ball as Sanjay and I took the seats Claudia had saved for us in the second row.

We found ourselves right next to Abhi, who was sitting next to Ben and his parents. Abhi smiled, but Ben barely gave me a glance. If that was how it was going to be, it was fine with me. I could pretend he didn't exist, too.

Abhi gestured at the row in front of us and whispered, "That's the Mackson family. Henry Mackson has a big part in the play. Claudia is friends with two of his sisters, and the youngest sister, Mimi, is in the grade below us. Their mom is from India; believe it or not, our grandfathers went to the same college!"

"That's wild," I said.

"I wish it could be me up on that stage. *Up and down, up and down, I will lead them up and down: I am feared in field and town: Goblin, lead them up and down*."

"Are you in plays at school?" I asked.

Abhi gave me a sad smile. "I wish. As it is, my dad feels like he's doing me a favor allowing me to play baseball. And I can't give that up."

I nodded. I didn't want to give up baseball, either. But I knew the time was coming when I'd have to.

"Shh," Ben said. "They're starting."

The play was awesome. The story was about a bunch of humans (including Claudia's character, Helena) who get caught in a fairy argument and become enchanted in hilarious ways. Because the stage was set at the edge of the forest, it felt like fairies really could just pop up at any minute. My skin tingled strangely as the thought crossed my mind. I rubbed my arms and made myself pay attention to the stage.

The best character in the whole play was Henry Mackson's

character, Puck, the lieutenant to the fairy king, Oberon. Puck was a mischief-maker who went by different names, including Robin Goodfellow, which had to be an even stranger name than Puck. Puck was super athletic, leaping and running onstage. He seemed like he'd make a great ballplayer, especially at shortstop or in the outfield.

I didn't like the way Oberon used Puck to force his queen and wife, Titania, into doing what he wanted by enchanting her into falling in love with a donkey-headed man (not to mention giving some poor guy a donkey head!). In fact, most of the female characters in the play had to deal with lots of nonsense from the males.

It wasn't that different from the real world, where I had to deal with boys who were resentful of girls playing baseball and being good at math. In the hours I'd already spent playing baseball on the Salt Shakers, no one but Abhi had much to say to me.

Titania had a bunch of fairies serving her—they were named strange things like Peaseblossom, Cobweb, Mustardseed, and Moth. But they were just side characters; none of them had actual personalities, like Puck. I didn't want to be a side character in anyone else's story. I wanted to star in my own.

Puck was in a tough position, though. He had to follow orders from the fairy king, Oberon. But when he realized he'd made a mistake and given a love potion to the wrong guy, he tried to fix it, and accidentally made things even worse. I didn't believe in luck or magic. But as the sun tipped below the horizon in a rainbow blaze and the first star appeared in the sky, I wished there were a magical being who would somehow fix my summer and help me find a landing spot in this town, who could help me unburden my secret to Ben so I could try out for the Math Puzzler team when school started.

During intermission, Sanjay went off to see if he could catch a glimpse of Claudia before she went back onstage. I got up to stretch my legs and found myself at the edge of the woods. Leaves and brush stirred in the darkening evening, and I thought about Rob, the odd boy Ben and I had met, the one who hit home runs and seemed as delighted by math as we were. I wondered what he was doing tonight, and whether he'd found a way to do what he loved most.

A large, pale moth landed on my hand like a whisper. I watched it for a moment, noting the spots on its wings like giant eyes.

"I wonder if we'll ever see Rob again?" came a voice behind me. The moth flew off into the night, and I turned to find Ben standing next to me peering into the woods.

It shouldn't have surprised me that looking at the woods made Ben think of Rob. "Didn't he mention a . . . restaurant, or something?" I asked.

"The Salt Shaker? It's brand-new, and super tiny. There's

always a line around the block, so I've never been inside," said Ben. He scratched his head. "I'd only stop in there to get Rob to play ball."

"It sounded like he wasn't going to play anymore this summer."

"Maybe we could change his mind and get him to give us some tips."

"It seems like he's not allowed to," I said.

Ben crossed his arms and scowled. "I suppose you wouldn't want him to, would you?"

I glared at him. "What's that supposed to mean? He said he had responsibilities. What do you want him to do, be your private coach all summer?"

Ben clenched his hands. "Just because *you* think you're so amazing doesn't mean *other* people don't want to improve."

"You don't need him," I said smoothly. "You just need to pay attention during practice."

Ben's mouth hung open for a moment. "I pay attention!"

I sniffed. "You're always goofing around with Abhi."

That was true, and he knew it.

"You're just jealous," Ben said.

That was also true, but I wasn't about to admit it.

We stormed off in opposite directions. I liked it better when he ignored me.

Chapter Six

Ben
The Thief

I had to admit that Claudia was right. The play was really fun.

But it also brought home to me that winning was everything. The fairies used magic and the humans used deception to get what they wanted. And it all ended up working out better for everyone.

I needed to do the same. Our team needed to start winning, and I needed to find a way to become a better player. Better than Trish. I couldn't lose to her at everything. The last time I'd played in a championship game, our team had lost because of me. And Dad. Dad believed I was better than I was, and kept putting pressure on me. And then, while we were distracted, the worst thing in the world had happened.

"You ought to give Trish a chance," Abhi said as we

waited for Claudia to come out after the play was finished. "You guys are like two sides of the same coin."

I looked at him with horror. "We are not!"

"You know, we just finished watching *A Midsummer Night's Dream*, but I feel like we're living *Much Ado About Nothing*."

"What's that supposed to mean?"

Abhi grinned. "It's another Shakespeare play about two stubborn people who have lots in common but refuse to be together, so they need their friends to help them."

He was living one of his Shakespearean fantasies again. "Whatever, dude."

"*Let me be that I am and seek not to alter me*," said Abhi. Then his eyes widened. "Don't look now, but Home Run Kid is here," he murmured.

"Rob? What? Where?" I craned my neck to scan the area.

"Don't make it too obvious that we're looking," said Abhi. "Eight o'clock."

I turned my head casually. It was Rob! He was bareheaded for once, his hair shining in the moonlight. He was with the silver-haired man again, as well as a girl whose light hair glinted green. The three of them seemed to be arguing about something. At least, the old man kept talking while Rob shook his head and the girl stood with her arms crossed. Eventually, the old man stopped, the girl put her hands on her hips, and Rob looked down and clenched his jaw.

And then I was almost sure he looked up at me and held my gaze for a long moment before turning back to the man.

"Did you see that?" I whispered to Abhi. "Rob—"

"That was so much fun," came a voice. "Claudia did a great job."

Trish. Of course. She always had the worst timing. "How come you're still here?" I asked. Sure, it was rude, but I couldn't help it.

"Sanjay's still waiting for Claudia to come out," Trish said.

"How's your wrist doing?" Abhi asked.

This made me feel like a complete jerk. I should have been the one asking that, since I was the one who'd hurt Trish, accident or no accident.

Trish held up her wrist, which was no longer taped up. She moved it around in a complete circle and didn't even wince. "Believe it or not, it doesn't hurt at all," she said. "It began to feel better right after the game last Sunday. The swelling's gone, too. I should be able to pitch next week."

She healed fast! Or maybe the sprain wasn't as bad as everyone thought? I looked up to see what Rob was doing, but he and the old man were gone.

"Where'd Rob and his dad go?" I asked Abhi. "They were with a green-haired girl."

He shook his head. "No idea. One minute they were

standing at the edge of the woods, and the next minute they disappeared."

I exhaled loudly. I wanted to talk to Rob again, without Trish around this time. "Let's look for him," I said to Abhi.

"Your parents told us to stay here so we can leave right after Claudia comes out. But we can keep an eye out," Abhi said. "And you guys can discuss plans for the Math Puzzler team or something."

I scowled. "What do you mean?"

"Well, you two are going to be the stars of the team, right?" He looked back and forth between Trish and me.

Trish didn't say anything, but her dark eyes bored into me like she could see right into my brain, into my heart and all the worry and fear that sat there. She'd given me a look like that at the Math Puzzler tournament, right before she beat me for the top prize.

"Don't assume anything," I said to Abhi. "She hasn't even tried out for the team."

"Have you solved my problem yet?" asked Trish, raising her eyebrows.

From her expression, she already knew the answer to that question. "Let's get out of here," I muttered to Abhi. The heat rose in my face, and I moved away.

"Can you believe her?" I said.

But Abhi hadn't followed me. I looked back, and he was still standing at the edge of the woods, deep in conversation with my nemesis.

It wasn't enough that Trish embarrassed me at the Math Puzzler tournament and on the baseball field.

Now she was stealing my best friend.

Chapter Seven

Trish

Twin Trouble

The next day, we lost another game, even though Mike started the game and pitched well. He gave up just one run, but our team only got two hits, and we couldn't score. We may have been named the Salt Shakers, but we played like flat sodas. Ben still avoided me like I had a disease, and no one else had much to say, either. But Abhi had invited me to his house to practice pitching. He said his mom could pick me up on the way home from his sisters' dance practice during the week. And so here she was at our house, trailing twin girls.

Mom was at the hospital, so Dad greeted Abhi's mom at the door. "Thanks so much for having Trish over, Sujata."

"It's our pleasure to have Trish come to our home," said Abhi's mom. She had a slight accent, unlike my parents, who were both born and raised in the U.S. "Abhi is happy, of course, but so are the girls."

The twins, who were nine, looked exactly alike—the same thick wavy hair, same sparkling brown eyes, same sly smiles. One wore a blue T-shirt and black shorts, and the other had on a red shirt and jean shorts. They were a few inches shorter than me, thin and wiry and twittering like birds.

"I'm Aadya," said the blue-shirted one with a grin.

"I'm Asha," said the red-shirted one with an identical grin.

"Abhi doesn't usually invite girls over," said Aadya.

"We're practicing pitching," I said.

"Oh, we know," said Asha.

I got the funny feeling they knew almost everything.

"Take it easy throwing today," said Dad. "Don't wear out your arm." My wrist had healed just fine and didn't even twinge when I did push-ups, but Dad always made sure I didn't overdo things and hurt myself.

"We're just having a catch and working on changeups, nothing too strenuous."

"Okay. Have fun," Dad said. "See you around nine."

We made our way to their SUV and Asha opened a door for me. I climbed in and found myself in the middle seat with a twin to either side. We buckled up, and the girls started asking questions.

"Where'd you move from?" asked Aadya.

"Abhi said New Hampshire," said Asha.

"Yes, but where in New Hampshire?" asked Aadya.

"As if you know enough about New Hampshire to understand her answer," said Asha.

They went on this way for quite a while. It was confusing at first, but I was also relieved that I didn't have to answer all their rapid-fire questions.

"Trish? Trish?" asked Asha.

I blinked and turned to her. "Yeah?"

"Do you like our bracelets? We made them ourselves," said Aadya. She stuck out a bony wrist and showed off a bracelet made of pink, purple, and yellow threads knotted and braided together in a complex pattern.

"It's really nice," I said truthfully.

"Look at mine," said Asha. It had three different colors in the same pattern.

"So cool. I make them, too." I showed her my bracelet, a faded rainbow of strings. A pang of loneliness stabbed at me. I'd made identical ones for my whole baseball team back home in South Ridgefield. I'd only been there for two years, and I'd finally bonded with my team. Now this was all I had left of them, except for memories.

"Would you like to make some bracelets with us?" asked Asha.

"Oh, I—"

"It won't take long," said Aadya. "We can show you some

new patterns, maybe. And you can teach us something, too." She shook her wrist again.

"Sure, if there's time after Abhi and I—"

"Oh, you'll have time before," said Asha.

We pulled into a garage. "Here we are," said Abhi's mom.

We went into the mudroom off the garage where we all took off our shoes.

"Come to our room," said Aadya, pulling on my arm.

"But Abhi—"

"Abhi won't be finished yet," said Asha. "He's with Daddy. Come on."

I let them lead me through the kitchen, which smelled like a delicious combination of caramelized onions and spices, upstairs to the back of the house where we came to a bedroom with pink and yellow walls, white furniture, and two beds with pink and yellow blankets.

"Here's the table . . ." Asha led me to a round table covered in art supplies and thread.

". . . where we make our bracelets!" said Aadya. She pulled out a stool and pushed me onto it.

"What colors would you like?" asked Asha.

"Uh . . ." I looked around, hoping Abhi might be lurking in a corner. They clearly weren't going to let me leave the room until I'd made a bracelet. "How about . . . green, blue, and white?"

"Salt Shakers colors, huh?" Asha seemed disappointed.

"Yes, why not?" I said.

"Baseball, baseball. You sound like Abhi," said Aadya.

"Well, I love baseball." My voice rose defensively.

"That's okay," said Asha, giggling. "But what else do you love?"

"Well . . . math."

"Ooh! Like Ben," said Aadya. "We love Ben!"

Hmm. Ben wasn't that easy to love. Or like. Or tolerate for the length of a baseball game. "You do?"

"Of course," said Asha. "He's always sweet to us. And he's been Abhi's best friend since forever."

Aadya picked out four different colors and started cutting them into equal lengths. "And Ben's so cute," she giggled.

It was hard to see past his permanent scowl, though.

"And so smart," gushed Asha.

There was no doubt about that!

"Don't you think Ben's awesome? I bet you two are great friends, since you like all the same things," Aadya said while Asha finished knotting and taping eight threads to the table in front of me—two each of green, blue, white, and black.

"Oh, I wouldn't exactly say that," I said.

Both girls stopped working on their bracelets and stared at me.

"I . . . I mean, Ben's fine, I guess." I had to end this

conversation. "Can you show me how to make the patterns you guys are wearing?"

"Yes!" said Asha. "It's called a broken ladder pattern. You should be able to do it, since you're already an advanced bracelet maker."

The twins showed me how to start with a normal chevron pattern first, and then take strings and tie knots to form a "spiral staircase," then repeat the chevron with the next set of colors. They were right—it was surprisingly easy. And their chattering didn't bother me as much when I was concentrating on making my bracelet.

If only it was as easy to weave friendships as it was to make these.

"Hey," Abhi said from the doorway.

"Hi, big brother," said Aadya. "Did Daddy finally let you go?"

Abhi fiddled with the doorframe. "Yeah, I'm done," he said. "Ready to go, Trish?"

I left my half-finished bracelet on the table and rushed to join Abhi, but then turned back. "Thank you," I said to the twins. "That was fun. Maybe I can finish it later?" I hurried to follow Abhi out the door.

We went out to the yard, and Abhi and I worked on making our pitching motions for our circle changeups look exactly like our fastballs.

"How'd you learn to pitch so well?" he asked.

"My brother Sanjay," I said. "He's played ball all his life. He says having excellent mechanics would help make up for the fact that I'd never be the strongest person on the field. It makes my pitches hard to hit, no matter how big a batter's muscles are."

"Well, I'll never be the strongest on the field, either," said Abhi. "If I can learn how to do this, it will really help me, too."

We pitched for a while, and then practiced fielding pop-ups by throwing the ball straight in the air. My wrist didn't even ache. We took a break and drank some water.

"Thanks for having me over," I said. "This is fun."

"You're an awesome player," said Abhi. "And you're cool."

To my horror, tears sprang to my eyes. "Thanks," I said, trying to avoid blinking. "It's . . . it's been a tough few weeks. It's not easy moving to a new place."

Abhi nodded and looked out at his yard. "I can imagine. But Comity's a great town. Lots of famous people have come from here, you know, like authors and singers and even a celebrity chef. But no famous baseball players that I know of. Or mathematicians, come to think of it." He grinned. "Maybe you'll be the first of both! Everyone's psyched you're on our team this summer."

I snorted. Abhi might be psyched, but I wasn't sure that meant "everyone" was. "It's not helping us win, is it?"

Abhi shrugged. "We've both watched and played enough

baseball to know that sometimes great players, and even great teams, go through rough patches. We're going to get there, I know it. And Ben . . . I know he's been acting weird. But don't hold it against him; he's been through a lot."

"Yeah?" I leaned forward. If anyone could explain Ben, it would be his best friend.

Abhi scratched the back of his neck. "He likes you." Abhi glanced at the ground, then back up at me.

"What?" He could have told me that Ben was secretly the star of the New England Turkeys, and it would have surprised me less.

Abhi nodded. "Really. He likes you. As a friend, I mean. He told me. He just doesn't know how to show you."

Could that possibly be true? Abhi wouldn't make that up, would he? I studied him briefly, but he didn't break out laughing or tell me it was just a bad joke.

Suddenly, the whole world seemed different.

Abhi's mom came out to the yard wiping her hands on her apron. "Abhi, Trish, please come in. Dinner is ready."

"But we were just about to start pitching again," Abhi said.

"You will still have plenty of daylight after dinner," she said, walking back inside.

We went into the house. I put one foot in front of the other, but I couldn't feel them touch the ground.

Ben wanted to be my friend! All the crankiness, ignoring

me . . . it was just an act! Or, even if that was just his personality, it covered up the fact that Ben didn't actually detest me! Well, if he wanted to be my friend, I wanted to be his. We had so much in common, it only made sense!

Dinner was freshly made pooris, deep-fried, puffed, and steaming, and a savory potato sagu with onions and ginger. The food was hot and delicious, and it was fun to eat with our hands. Even Aadya and Asha were relatively silent as we all ate ravenously. I couldn't help thinking about Ben. What did Abhi mean, that he wasn't acting like himself? How could I get him to act the way he actually felt? Six pooris later, I was no closer to the answer, but I was definitely full. I sipped some water.

"So Trish, you are having a good time on the baseball team?" asked Abhi's dad.

"Oh, yes, Mr. Nair," I said, more hopefully than truthfully. "It's been fun."

"Please call us Uncle and Auntie," said Abhi's mom. Every Indian mom I'd ever met asked me to call her Auntie. It was like having a billion relatives I didn't know yet.

"Okay, Auntie," I said. "Thank you so much for the delicious dinner. My mom never makes pooris."

Abhi's mom laughed. "They are not the heart-healthiest food," she said. "But I'm glad you like them."

"Your brother's name is Sanjay?" Abhi's dad asked.

"Yes," I said.

"And your name? Are you named after—"

"It's not short for Patricia, it's short for Trisha," I said, pronouncing the T like a "th" and trilling the R.

"Trisha means 'thirst' or 'desire' in Sanskrit," said Abhi's dad, nodding.

"Mom said it was appropriate since I wanted to learn everything, even when I was little."

"And you are also on the Math Puzzler team?"

"Yes. Well, I was at my old school," I said.

"She won the tournament in April," said Abhi.

"My team didn't—"

"Your team came in third. But you got the highest individual score. You beat *Ben*," said Abhi.

That's what everyone thought. But I knew I hadn't beaten him. And if Ben found out, he'd be upset all over again. Abhi might change his mind about being friends, and Mom . . . I didn't want to think about how disappointed she'd be.

Abhi's dad tilted his head in a way that reminded me of Abhi. "Very impressive," he said. "What kind of study materials do you use?"

"Oh, my math textbooks, and every puzzle book I can get from the library," I said. "The thing is, it's not only about math." I knew I shouldn't try out for the team next year, but oh how I wanted to.

"Maybe you could share some of these with Abhi.

Anything to get his math grades up," said Abhi's dad. "I've been working with him every evening, but he's not making much progress."

My mouth dried up. Did Abhi's dad actually say that in front of everyone? Mom, whatever faults she had, would never embarrass me on purpose like that. Aadya and Asha chattered on like nothing had happened. I took another sip of water, spilled some on my shirt, and tried to blot it quickly.

Abhi turned to me. "Are you done? Let's get back out there while we still have daylight. Okay, Mom?"

Abhi's mom nodded. "Yes, Abhi. Just leave your plates in the sink, please."

I picked up my empty plate and followed Abhi into the kitchen.

"I hate it when he does that," he said, putting his plate in the sink and washing his hands.

"I'm sorry, I didn't mean to—"

"You didn't do anything. I just have to live with the fact that nothing will ever matter to him as much as math. I need it for engineering, he says. Only I don't want to be an engineer. And the only thing I'm good at is baseball. And English. Well, memorizing Shakespeare, at least. *There was a star danced, and under that was I born.*"

I spoke in a low voice. "I know how you feel. My mom says she's glad that this season will be over soon and that'll be the end of my playing baseball. But all I can think about is how much I love it, and how much I'll miss it. How come parents don't see us, just some make-believe image of what they think we're supposed to be?"

Abhi raised his eyebrows. "Wait a minute. You're quitting after this season? Why?"

Wasn't it obvious? "Well, because . . . because we move up to the big field in the spring, and I won't be able to keep up."

"You don't seem to have trouble keeping up now," Abhi said. "You're one of the best players on our team."

I shook my head. "You don't understand."

Abhi furrowed his brow. "You sound like Ben. I understand more than you think."

"It's not easy, okay? Giving up baseball and the Math Puzzler team."

"You're giving up the Math Puzzler team, too? After you beat Ben to win the Individual Prize?" Abhi asked incredulously.

I sighed. "Let's get some more throws in before the sun goes down."

We went into the yard again. The sun hung low in the sky, but we still had a good hour before it would set. We threw the ball back and forth easily for a while.

Maybe I could tell Abhi what was weighing on me, and he'd help me figure out how to explain it to Ben. Now that I knew

Ben wanted to be friends, maybe he wouldn't hate me forever. "I was more shocked than anyone when I won the Individual Prize," I started. "And actually—"

"Dude!" came a voice. "I know you said you were busy for dinner, but do you have time to practice now? If I'm ever going to get better, I need your help."

I froze. It was *Ben*!

He coasted to a stop on his bike and leaned it against the side of the house. He hadn't seen me yet; I tried to smile in a casual, friendly, yet not awkward way.

Ben suddenly noticed me and took a step back. "What's she doing here?"

He has a hard time showing he cares, I thought.

"We've been working on our changeups," said Abhi.

"Couldn't you do that during practice?"

There's a double meaning in that! Maybe he wants me to practice pitching with him, too? I continued to smile encouragingly.

Abhi shrugged. "Like you said, we need more practice. Besides, I thought it would be fun to have Trish over."

Ben glowered. "She's the reason you were busy for dinner? Anything else I should know about? Planning any family vacations?"

"Come on, dude," said Abhi. "Chill. You've had dinner at our house millions of times. We can all be friends."

"Want to hang out for a while? We can all practice together,"

I said, trying desperately to keep my voice from quavering.

But Ben got back on his bike and took off down the street.

Once I arrived home, I plopped myself at the kitchen table, taped my half-finished string bracelet to the table, and worked on completing it. Was all of Ben's awkwardness just masking how he really felt about me? Was that why he was jealous of my friendship with Abhi?

"Did you have fun at Abhi's house?" Mom was away from her laptop, for once, and came into the kitchen to refill her water glass.

"Yeah," I said, knotting a green thread in place.

"I knew you'd make friends easily."

"Nothing about this move has been easy. Just like all the other moves we've made."

Mom said nothing for a moment while I continued working on the bracelet. Blue thread now.

"I used to make those when I was a kid. Can I see?"

"Sure," I said. I stopped tying knots and made a mental note of what string was next.

"My friends and I also used to braid different colored ribbons into hair barrettes and wear different ones depending on what outfit we were wearing." Mom chuckled.

My breathing got tight. "Well, I don't have any friends who

wear barrettes, so that's not something I would be doing," I said.

"I didn't mean you should—"

"And I don't even have hair that I could wear a barrette in," I said, my voice cracking.

"Well, Trish, you're the one who decided to cut—"

"It's late. I should go to bed," I said. I grabbed the bracelet and stood.

"Wait," said Mom. She took a large white envelope off the counter and handed it to me. "This came for you."

I glanced at the envelope, and my heart plummeted like my sinking fastball. It was from the Math Puzzler Championship organizers, I knew it.

"What is it?"

"Just a catalog, I'm sure. Good night, Mom." I turned and ran upstairs to my room.

Once there, I opened the envelope with trembling hands. The Math Puzzler people had finally discovered the mistake, and now everyone would find out. I knew it would catch up to me eventually. And Ben would hate me even more, and Mom would be so upset.

But it wasn't a letter with bad news. It wasn't a letter at all.

It was a slim booklet bound in soft leather with a curious pattern stamped into it. *The Mathematics of The Wild* was printed on the first page in a flowing font. Then below it, *The solutions lead to the ultimate answer.*

I opened it. Weirdly, most of the pages were blank. What a waste of space! But when I flipped to the second page, I found a puzzle.

I examined the envelope again. There was no return address, not even a postmark. Had someone just put it in my mailbox? Who would have done that?

Who else in town loved math like me? *Ben.* Could it be him? Was this his way of showing he cared?

The puzzle was interesting. So I started working on solving it.

Chapter Eight

Ben
The Puzzle

I rode home in a fog of fury. Trish really was stealing my best friend! How could Abhi fall for it? Trish was obnoxious, devious . . . and that crazy math problem! I still couldn't solve it. I could probably search for the answer on the internet, but I wouldn't give Trish the satisfaction. Maybe it was a trick. Maybe it wasn't a solvable problem. But somehow I knew that wasn't true. And I knew I'd better have the answer soon, or I'd never live it down.

I got to my house and slammed my brakes. I had an idea.

If math could make me feel calmer about baseball, maybe baseball could make me feel calmer about math.

I snuck past Fib, who was napping in the kitchen and didn't stir when I slid open the door to the backyard. I couldn't practice batting with no one else around, but I could definitely do some throwing and maybe even some pitching. I went to the shed, where we had a target, like a vertical trampoline, that I could throw against. I dragged it onto the grass, brushing cobwebs off my face.

Moving the target had revealed the old equipment bag from two years ago. I started to get a queasy feeling in my stomach. I hadn't seen it since that last game.

I reached inside, felt around, and grabbed a ball. I took it outside into the waning sunshine, and then caught my breath. Dad's baseball, the gift our team had given him right before the championship game two years ago to thank him for coaching. I turned it around, slowly tracing the signatures written in blue Sharpie. It was from the last game I'd played before this summer, that last disastrous game in the spring of fourth grade.

I found my signature. I'd been so full of hope then, hope that I could contribute to our team's victory. Instead, I'd messed up as a pitcher and a batter and had single-handedly lost the championship for our team. Dad said it wasn't all my fault, and he was right. It was also his. And in the aftermath of that, we lost Grandma Beth.

But now maybe I didn't have to be terrible. Maybe I could at least be average. I gripped the ball and stood. I'd start with short throws, and then work my way farther back.

I threw at the target, managed to hit it, and caught the

ball when it bounced back to me. Not so bad. I took a couple of steps back and did it again. I kept backing up, throwing, and catching. I'd grown, and baseball felt different, but it was almost like seeing an old friend again after years apart. I considered the ball in my hand again. Maybe I could try pitching, just to see how it felt. I wouldn't be good enough to pitch for our team, but it might be good to work out my arm.

I moved to what I estimated was the right distance and practiced my windup. *Balance first*, as Grandma Beth liked to say. I didn't have any fancy moves, and I was sure I didn't look like I was born to pitch, like Trish or Abhi, but I managed to stand on my left foot and pick up my right without falling over, which was more than I expected. After doing that a few times, I figured it was time to release the ball.

As I wound up and leaned back, the back door slid open and a brown flash streaked into the yard. That was enough to distract me, and I threw the ball way wide of the target and into the shrubs that bordered the woods. I let out a frustrated breath.

"Hey, Ben!" called Dad as he stepped into the yard. "Pitching again, huh?"

Fib had reached me by then and gave my hand a quick lick before he went over to sniff at something in the bushes.

"I'm just fooling around. I'm not pitching this summer."

Dad rubbed his hands together. "What do you want to

work on? Batting or fielding? I've got some drills I want to run with the team this week."

His smile reminded me of Grandma Beth's, wide and kind and reaching all the way to his eyes. A smile that made me feel like anything might be possible. Almost.

But I didn't want him constantly telling me what to do like he used to. My stomach began to rumble. "I was about to stop. I've been out here a while."

"Come on, let's practice together. I noticed your swings aren't really level. You need to use the power in your legs, or you'll never hit anything out of the infield. And your fielding could use some work, too. Let's start by having a catch."

"I'm tired, Dad," I lied. I didn't want to play ball with him. He both reminded me and didn't remind me of Grandma, and either way it was too painful. I stared at the ground as the silence stretched between us. As the moments ticked by I glanced at Dad, and I could see him struggling with what to say.

"Okay, maybe next time," said Dad slowly. "Can I give you a hand putting this stuff away?"

"Sure." As long as Dad didn't realize I'd been using his special game ball, I should be able to escape without a lecture.

We stowed the throwing target in the shed, and I put away my glove. I turned around and found Fib with the ball in his mouth, shifting his eyes between me and Dad and wagging his tail. "Bring it here, Fib," I said, holding my hand out. I shouldn't have been using that ball. I had to get it before Dad recognized it.

But Fib just watched me and mouthed the ball some more.

"Come on, Fib. Give it," I said, standing taller.

"Drop it," said Dad, trying to grab the ball. But Fib danced around him and ran to stand at the edge of our yard with his back to the woods.

Fib's tongue lolled and his tail wagged slowly. His bright brown eyes stared into mine like he was trying to tell me something. "Fib—"

He turned and raced into the woods.

"Fib!" I called after him. After a few moments waiting, I knew he wasn't going to return on his own. What had gotten into him lately? I turned to Dad. "I'd better go. Remember how long it took to find him last week after our game?"

"I'll come with you," said Dad.

I shook my head. "That's okay. I'll be back soon."

I ran into the woods before he had a chance to say anything else.

I jogged on the path toward Bailey Park. The sun hadn't set yet, but as the trees grew closer together, the light dimmed and the woods around me seemed to whisper in a language I couldn't quite understand. Goose bumps erupted on my arms and neck. "Fib!" I called. "Come here!"

But Fib was nowhere in sight.

I kept running on the path in the waning light, hoping I'd get to Fib before it got dark. Where in the world had he gone? I approached two droopy evergreens and took a moment to catch my breath.

Something rustled in the brush nearby. Sure enough, it was Fib with the baseball in his mouth, wagging his entire back end furiously.

"There you are! Drop it," I said.

Fib dropped the ball at my feet and sat wearing a big doggy smile with green dust all over his muzzle. The spiral pattern on his head seemed to glow in the twilight.

I picked up the ball and examined it. It was beat-up and covered in grass stains. There were no signatures.

I held it out to Fib. "This is the wrong one," I said. "Where's Dad's ball?"

Fib panted and swished his tail. He turned toward home and looked back at me hopefully.

"So now you want to go home? But I've got to keep looking for it!"

I searched for the baseball in the undergrowth, with Fib snuffling next to me, until it became too dim to search anymore. I reached my hand under one last bush in a desperate attempt to salvage something from this strange evening. Still no sign of Dad's ball.

It had been our team's gift to Dad, the only good thing that had happened that night two years ago. And I had lost it, just like I'd lost the game for our team that night. And we'd lost Grandma Beth.

I was so tired of losing.

After a few more minutes groping in the bushes, I finally gave up.

"Come on, Fib." We ran home on the path, Fib leading the way eagerly.

"Hey Ben," Dad said as I entered the kitchen. "Something came for you." He handed me a white envelope with my name on it but no return address.

Well, that was strange. I ripped it open and pulled out something.

It was a book. It had a worn leather cover with indentations that formed a decorative pattern.

I flipped through its pages. Most of them were blank. But the first page said:

THE MATHEMATICS

OF

THE WILD

The solutions lead to the ultimate answer.

Intrigued, I turned the page.

There was a puzzle!

			T		**A**
E		**P**	**S**		
	T				
L					**P**
	E			**T**	

I smiled. It was a kind of logic puzzle, like sudoku. It wasn't a matter of calculating anything, just putting the letters in the right positions so they didn't repeat in any row, column, or rectangle of six. I squinted at the puzzle. This would be easy to solve, but I needed to get upstairs.

"What is it?" asked Dad.

"Just a math book," I said, shoving it back in the envelope. "I'm heading up to bed. Good night."

I took the stairs two at a time to my room while Fib scrambled up beside me, his nails clicking on the wood.

I grabbed a pencil from my desk and scrawled my answers.

S	P	E	**T**	L	**A**
T	A	L	P	S	E
E	L	**P**	**S**	A	T
A	**T**	S	E	P	L
L	S	T	A	E	**P**
P	**E**	A	L	**T**	S

The entire grid turned bright green. I stared at it, blinking for a few moments, but it stayed green.

Then, under the puzzle, a sentence appeared:

Say it out loud.

I ran my hand over my eyes. I was seeing things. How was that possible? And what the heck did that mean? Where did this book come from, anyway?

Suddenly, it hit me. I knew who had sent me the book.

It was *Rob*. He knew I loved math, and he knew I needed help with baseball. Was the "ultimate answer" the book mentioned about baseball? And could this book help me solve Trish's math problem?

Fib leaned against my leg and put his head in my lap. I traced the soft white spiral on his head and a sense of calm came over me. I stared out my window to the darkening woods.

"Nothing to do but try it." I glanced around like someone might be playing a joke on me, but of course there was no one in the room but me and Fib. I took out the crumpled sheet of paper with Trish's puzzle:

1 11 21 1211 111221 312211

I said the numbers out loud.

And suddenly, after more than a week of being stumped, everything clicked into place. I wrote my answer carefully, whispering the numbers to myself.

I flipped the page in the math book and found that another puzzle had appeared.

But it wasn't like any math puzzle I'd ever seen.

It was a poem.

In times or division, it's always the same.
Unus and ein, as victors proclaim.
The lonely, the only, the solo, the sun.
The foxglove, the skullcap, the answer is ____.

What the heck did that mean?

My phone rang, startling me. It was Abhi.

"Dude," I said.

"Dude," said Abhi. "Why'd you run off like that?"

I was too happy about finding the mysterious math book and finally solving Trish's puzzle to be too cranky about this evening. "I just thought it was weird that you'd invite Trish and not me," I said.

"Dude, that's just it," said Abhi. "Trish needed to tell me what she couldn't tell you."

"What?" My stomach started to feel queasy again.

"She likes you, Ben. As a friend, I mean. But she's too intimidated to know how to act with you."

"Trish? Intimidated by *me*? What are you even talking about?" Trish had already proven she was better than me at both math and baseball.

"She knows you're super smart, and she's trying hard to be a good teammate this summer. She wants to be friends, Ben. She feels she started on the wrong foot with you and doesn't know how to make it better. And you have to admit that you've been pretty harsh to her."

He was right. I *had* been harsh. "She . . . she thinks I'm smart?"

"Everyone knows you're smart. Trish was just as shocked by her Math Puzzler win as you were."

I didn't answer. Could it be true? Abhi was my best friend in the world, and he wouldn't lie to me.

"Ben? Are you there?"

"Yeah," I said. My chest lightened, like ropes were finally loosening. If Trish wanted to be friends, I certainly wasn't going to say no! She was a math goddess, and the best player on our team by a long shot. We had so much in common. It felt like fate. "But I've been such a jerk to Trish. How can I make it up to her?"

"Just be kind. She doesn't know anyone else and could use some good friends."

"Kind?" I said stupidly. Trish didn't hate me, but maybe she should. I'd messed everything up.

"Yeah. Like with your actions. And your words," Abhi said.

"Okay, I'll try," I said. I took a deep breath. "It's been a long day. I'd better go to sleep. I'll call you tomorrow."

Abhi hung up. Fib took his head off my lap, jumped on the bed, and curled up.

It *had* been a long day. I closed the magical book (What else could explain what was happening?) and put it away in my nightstand drawer.

Then I changed into pajamas and climbed into bed next to Fib, letting his furry, solid warmth relax me.

As I closed my eyes, I smiled.

Say it out loud meant something completely different to me now.

Chapter Nine

Trish

The Salt Shaker

The puzzle had been a sudoku-like grid using letters instead of numbers: R I S L A P.

I'd solved it quickly, and to my shock, at the bottom of the page, a sentence materialized:

Show a sign.

I didn't know what kind of sophisticated invisible ink this booklet had, but it was mighty impressive. But it had promised "answers," not another cryptic clue. If this book was from Ben, what was he playing at? I thought more about it and realized that maybe this applied to me and what I was struggling with at the moment. Maybe Ben wanted me to show him a sign—a sign that I wanted to be friends.

I had the perfect idea.

I turned the page, and another puzzle had appeared. And it was a *poem*.

This was going to take some thought.

The next Saturday I went into Comity Town Center before our afternoon game. I was going to pitch today for the first time since my wrist injury, and a walk was a good distraction from my nerves. I decided to check out the Salt Shaker, which had a line going out the door and down the block. I'd noticed that Ben liked potato chips, so maybe I could get him a snack. Besides, my curiosity got the best of me as I wondered what could possibly make this place have such a cult following.

Luckily, the line moved fast. Ahead of me were two boys from another Comity baseball team, Margherita's Pizza Players.

"Look at the board up there and make sure you know your order ahead of time," said one.

"Why?" asked the other.

"Because if you don't know what you want when you get to the front of the line, and you don't spit it out right away, you have to get back in line again."

"No way!"

I leaned in to listen more closely. That was weird!

"Yeah. They say the line has to move fast, and if you hold it up you need to get out. But the food's so good, it's totally worth it."

I rolled my eyes. How good could it be?

As I got closer to the entrance, I saw the menu displayed on a neon green sign:

Spicy Sports Crisps

Team Spirit Truffle Fries

Morale-Boosting Mint Crackers

Arithmetic Avocado Toast

No-Guessing Gingko Pretzels

Concentration Cumin Biscuits

Pump-It-Up Plantain Chips

That had to be the strangest menu I'd ever seen. Judging from the number of baseball and soccer uniforms in line, the Sports Crisps seemed popular.

The tinted glass door to the store slid open, and the boys ahead of me stepped in. The door slid closed again right in front of my nose. There was no handle; I guessed it must be automatic.

A minute later, the door opened, and I stepped into the Salt Shaker.

It was tiny, barely big enough for a half-dozen customers to stand. It was decorated in stripes of bright green, cool blue, and white. Customers waited in an orderly line at a counter, and a bunch of young employees leaped around, taking orders from stammering customers, cooking food with brisk efficiency, and sliding trays with perfect timing.

A blue-haired teenage boy addressed me. "Pray tell, what

is your order? Please be quick. Just spit it out, and hurry. Don't be thick."

"S-Sports Crisps, please," I said. "And a lemonade?"

He raised a sarcastic eyebrow. "Aha. Is that a question, or a statement? Perhaps I should return you to the pavement?"

"A s-statement," I said. Why was I so nervous? And why was he talking in such a weird way? "Sports Crisps and a lemonade."

He held out his hand and I gave him a ten-dollar bill. He gave me my change immediately, like he already knew what I was going to order and had just been waiting for me to confirm.

"Young lady, off you go then, please wait there. Stay quiet, mind your business, don't you stare." He motioned to a spot next to a short line of other people waiting patiently at the counter. The two baseball boys were there, and they weren't talking.

I went over to my spot. It was easy not to talk, but I had to admit it was challenging not to stare.

The guys who worked in the kitchen were moving in a kind of complicated dance. They sliced, fried, sprinkled, and bagged the food, tossed it to others who double-checked the orders, then lobbed them to the ones at the counter, who slid the orders on bright green trays to stop exactly in front of the correct customer. It was amazing. It was beautiful. It was kind of impossible. And it happened with minimal talking, so you could hear the hiss of chips being lowered into the fryer and the slide of the trays across the counter. I was mesmerized by the process. It was like being inside a complicated, well-oiled machine.

My old baseball and Math Puzzler teams were like that. We knew each other's strengths and weaknesses and worked together to succeed. And if Ben and I were friends, maybe that could happen here, too.

The two Pizza Players got their orders. I stepped to the left and waited for mine.

The tray with my potato chips and lemonade slid toward me. But instead of stopping perfectly at the end of the counter like everyone else's, it kept going at an impressive speed, crashed into the short wall behind the counter, and toppled, soaking the front of my uniform shirt with lemonade. Red chips skittered across my chest, leaving a trail of streaks that made me look like I'd been clawed by a wild animal.

I gasped. Every eye in the store turned to me. Was I supposed to stop the tray? No one else had touched theirs until it had come to a complete stop.

"Basil!" cried the blue-haired order taker. "What happened? Have you gone completely mental? Or do you need reminders to be gentle?"

A purple-haired boy blushed. "I was asked to—"

"I've got this, Ivy, never fear," came another voice. The

speaker nodded to Basil, who stepped back into the kitchen. The person then hopped over the counter, and to my horror, came to me.

"I'm Luna, the assistant manager. Are you all right?" She looked a little older than me and spoke quietly in an accent I didn't recognize.

"I'm a mess," I said.

"We'll take care of that right now," said Luna, who had pale green hair that reached her shoulders and astounding eyes that were yellow, like a cat's. She took me by the elbow and brought me behind the counter. "We need to clean that shirt as soon as possible."

I shook my head. "I don't have time before my game."

"Don't worry," said Luna. "We'll have you cleaned up in no time. Ivy!" She glanced at her watch and addressed the blue-haired order taker, "Please inform our guests waiting in line that there will be a ten-minute delay. They will also receive ten percent off their orders." Ivy gave a quick nod and went outside.

Before I knew what was happening, Luna led me to a small bathroom, where I stripped off my sodden uniform shirt.

"I have a clean shirt here you can use while we take care of yours," called Luna through the door.

"I don't need it, thanks." Luckily, my tee underneath had been left unscathed.

I handed my sopping, stained uniform shirt to Luna, and she passed it to an orange-haired boy, who took it with a bow. Then Luna motioned for me to sit at a small table tucked into a corner of the kitchen. On it was a brand-new order of chips and lemonade. The kitchen was back to quiet efficiency, and I swore I could hear some of the guys humming.

"In addition to being the assistant manager, I'm the new chief scientist here at the Salt Shaker."

I looked at her in confusion.

"Not only do I train the staff, I concoct the recipes," said Luna. "Although, there appears to be a small issue today." A brief grimace crossed her face. "Anyway, I'm the one who makes this the most profitable shop in town, the one that will surely lead us to victory and allow us to . . ." she trailed off and glanced at me sideways.

"Allow you to what? And what victory?" I asked as I munched on the chips.

She laughed. "Never mind. You like them?"

I nodded and held one up. "I can see why people stand in line for these." They were pretty spicy, but quite tasty. The more I ate, the more I wanted to eat. "I sometimes help my parents cook, but it's more about speed than inspiration with them."

"Would you happen to know a way to make a savory treat more tart?"

I blinked. "Lime, maybe? Or vinegar?"

Luna shook her head. "We can't add liquid, it will make everything too soggy."

I thought for a moment about making chaat with Mom. What was that stuff again? "How about amchoor powder? It's made from unripe mango, so it's plenty tart."

"Oh, yes!" Luna appeared delighted and made a note in a small notebook she pulled from her pocket. "So other than cooking and baseball, what else do you like to do?"

To my surprise, I found myself opening up to Luna about math, and baseball, and the move.

"A math whiz and a baseball player? That's quite the combination."

I shrugged. "It doesn't make it any easier to make friends, especially as a girl surrounded by boys."

"Ah, you don't quite have a circle of friends yet?"

I shook my head. My eyes stung. I couldn't figure out why it was so easy to talk about all these feelings with a complete stranger when I couldn't talk to my own mom.

"I understand what it's like to be the only woman on a team." She waved at the kitchen. "It's not enough to be best at your job. You need to connect with your fellow players."

I sighed. "Boys can be so confusing."

"I know," said Luna seriously. "But if you show you're interested in what they have to say, they might open up a bit more."

"I try to talk to them about baseball," I said. "But it's still hard to—"

Luna smiled as the orange-haired boy came in. "Ah, thank you, Cricket. See, Trish? Here's your shirt, good as new."

I took my shirt from Cricket, and sure enough, it was clean and dry like it had never been splashed or stained. "How did you clean this so quickly?" I asked as I put it back on.

"We have our ways," Luna said with a wink. "Cooking can be a messy job. Here." She handed me what I'd paid for the chips and drink. "Everything's on the house for you today."

"Thank you," I said as I stood. "I need to get to my game now."

"Of course," Luna said. "What team should I root for?"

I laughed and turned around so she could see the back of my uniform. "Go, Salt Shakers!"

Luna's eyes widened, and she clapped her hands. "Of course!"

"Please do root for us. We could use all the help we can get."

Luna patted me on the shoulder. "Don't worry, Trish. Your friend problems are as good as solved. Everyone knows the real way to people's hearts. I'm hoping your team wins everything this summer. Just wish the same for me, okay?"

I wasn't sure what she was referring to, but she'd been so kind to me. "Of course," I said.

Luna gently guided me out the door. "Everything will

be fine." She smiled as she brushed a pale butterfly from my shoulder. "See? Good luck already."

As I walked toward Bailey Park, I realized I hadn't even bought any chips for Ben. My anxiety over ordering and the disaster with the lemonade had made me forget all about it.

I steeled myself. I could still show Ben a sign. If only I had the guts to do it.

Chapter Ten

Ben
The Homer

We arrived at Bailey Park to play our fifth game against another hulking Bridgeton team, Bob's Bowl-O-Rama Llamas. Our team was 0–4, the worst record in the league. I knew we'd lose again today, but I felt slightly hopeful thinking of the magical math book (Rob's?) and how it had helped me solve Trish's devious problem. Maybe some of that luck would rub off on my baseball playing, too?

Dad and I passed a small anthill in the Bailey parking lot. That wasn't typically something I'd notice, but the ants drew my eye today because they were forming a spiral as they crawled toward the peak.

A spiral, identical to the one the birds had formed at our first game.

It was another sign! But of what? I hope it didn't mean I'd injure another teammate.

We were walking toward the dugout when someone tapped me on the shoulder. I turned around to find Trish staring at me with her eyebrows all scrunched up. "Come with me for a second," she whispered.

Dad winked at me. He took my bag and kept going.

Did Trish know that I knew that she liked me? My feet stayed rooted to the ground.

"Come on," she said. "This'll only take a minute." She led me to the edge of the woods, glanced around us quickly, and took a deep breath. "I have something for you."

I swallowed. "You what?"

"I made you something. For luck."

I released the breath I'd been holding. I could use all the luck I could get.

"Hold out your arm," said Trish.

Everyone's heard of ice cream trucks. They're white, and display photos of different flavors of frozen treats, and play a cute little tune that draws kids for miles around.

I'd never heard of a snack truck. Certainly not one decked out in green, blue, and white with graffiti-like cartoons of different types of salty deliciousness.

But I sure heard it now, blasting hip-hop as it rolled into the Bailey parking lot. The truck drew quite a crowd. I hadn't had a chance to talk to Abhi yet about finding the math book last night, and certainly not about Trish in the woods today. And thanks to this snack truck, I wasn't going to get a chance now.

"Come get your spicy chips and fries and crackers," said the blue-haired driver as he opened the window and pointed to the menu on the outside of the truck. "Just grab and go, you'll love these salty snackers."

"Oh, man, truffle fries," said Abhi. He glanced at the truck. "And apparently they're good for building team spirit!"

The blue-haired guy continued. "Salt Shakers get free snacks, much as you wish. Just make sure to say thanks to teammate Trish."

"What?" Trish was buying snacks for the whole team? And why was that snack truck guy talking so strangely?

"This is great!" said Abhi, accepting some truffle fries and a bag of Sports Crisps. "Thanks, Trish."

"I met the assistant manager of the Salt Shaker. It must be her idea. It has nothing to do with me." Trish's voice shook.

"Sports Crisps?" asked Garrett. "What are those supposed to be?"

"Red crisps to make you strong and run so fast. They're spicy, but they'll get you really gassed!"

"That's ridiculous," said Garrett. "Chips can't make us better at baseball. Nothing can, as long we have Ben on our team."

Mike chuckled at his brother's joke, and my stomach did a slow roll. I hated to admit it, but he was right.

The driver shrugged and turned to the rest of the team. "And what say you, my bright and eager players? Don't pay attention to those sad naysayers."

"I'll take some Sports Crisps, please," said George. "Nice idea, Trish."

"Aren't you going to have some, Trish?" asked Abhi, munching on a fry. "These are delicious!"

"I just had a bunch at the Salt Shaker earlier," she said. "I'm sticking with water."

The Sports Crisps were kind of like super light potato chips. They were definitely spicy, in a kind of red-chili, cilantro way. They were also really tasty, but I couldn't see how they would make anyone more athletic.

The whole team was smiling, goofing around, and thanking Trish. She'd shown me that she wanted to be friends. But I felt a twinge of jealousy that our best player was getting even more attention, while everyone knew I couldn't bat my way out of a potato chip bag.

Was my luck ever going to change?

The Llamas were almost as gigantic and obnoxious as the Camemberts. During the first few innings I kept up my stellar .000 batting average, going 0 for 2, but at least I didn't drop any pop-ups or flub anything in the outfield. But Trish's pitching completely mystified the other team. I was grateful her injury hadn't made her rusty; she seemed to pitch as good as ever. We managed to keep it close. Very, very close.

In the bottom of the sixth, we were losing 1–0 with the tying run (Garrett) on second base and no outs. We had one last chance to win, but if we were true to form, we wouldn't find a way to do it.

George was up, then Campbell, then me. Unless there was a double play, I was going to have to bat. I might have a chance to lose the game for us. Or maybe, if my luck somehow changed, to win it.

George struck out swinging.

"Ben, you're on deck," called Abhi. I'd flipped my lucky coin looking for the best of fifty-one, and it came out twenty-six to twenty-five, heads. That gave me hope.

I stowed the coin, wiped my hands on my pants, and stood. My stomach did a backflip and I wasn't sure whether it was from anxiety or the Sports Crisps. Claudia would die laughing if I vomited on home plate. I let out a small burp. There, that was better.

I popped on a batting helmet, walked to the on-deck circle, and took a few practice swings. The bat felt lighter than usual. Maybe practicing was starting to pay off after all. Campbell hit a pop-up straight to the first baseman's glove, and I stepped up to home plate as he jogged back to the dugout.

I was potentially the last batter of the last inning. Garrett rolled his eyes at second base. It was clear what he was thinking: There was no way we were winning this game.

"It's Bombastic Ben!" yelled someone from the crowd. A bunch of people started cheering. What the heck? I stepped out of the batter's box to take a look.

It was the unibrowed goon pitcher from the Camemberts with his gigantic brother, Raccoon Face, and the rest of the team. Ugh.

"Let's see you smack one," taunted Raccoon Face.

"Or maybe step on your pitcher's wrist again," called Brick Wall to general applause.

I gritted my teeth. This was going to be even worse than I imagined, with the entire Camemberts team just waiting for me to fail so they could celebrate even more.

"Up to the plate, batter," said the ump.

I took a deep breath, stepped in the box again, and squared up. Suddenly, the advice from the math book popped into my head. *Say it out loud.*

"I want to get a hit," I murmured to myself.

I focused on the ball as the pitcher nodded to the catcher. I focused some more as he wound up. I squinted and focused with all my might as he let go. "Nice and slow," I whispered.

The ball flew toward me, but instead of landing in the

catcher's glove a split second later, it seemed to slow down. I didn't take my eyes off it. It was heading toward the outside of the plate, and it was surrounded by a sparkling green light. "Swerve into the strike zone," I whispered.

It was like looking through a magnifying glass. The baseball seemed larger than usual, and so slow I could see the seams as it spun. I brought the bat back. "Over the plate," I murmured as I pulled my hip around and kept my eye on that meatball of a strike as it drifted over home plate. My bat connected with a deafening ding and I followed all the way through on my swing. A jolt of lightning traveled up my arms.

Suddenly, the world went back to normal speed. The ball soared, still trailing faint green sparkles. It flew over the infield, and then the outfield, too. Out over the fence and onto Elm Street, where it bounced off the pavement.

"Ben, RUN!" Abhi yelled.

My legs moved mechanically, but I couldn't feel them. It was a home run. My first ever. My first hit this season.

A HOME RUN!

A walk-off homer to WIN THE GAME!

The crowd roared as I ran around the bases.

As I rounded third base, I leaped up to give Dad a high five, but I couldn't hear what he said over the cheering in the air. I came to home plate, where Garrett was waiting. I jumped on the plate with two feet, and our bench emptied and I was suddenly the center of a gigantic jumping mass of kids. "BEN! BEN! BOMBASTIC BEN!" they shouted, the insult now a cheer. David and Mike picked me up and set me on their shoulders, and the whole bunch of us paraded back to the dugout. Trish seemed as happy as the rest of the team; I guess she really did want to be my friend.

I couldn't calculate the odds of this happening. But I was elated anyway.

5

Chapter Eleven

Trish

The Ties That Bind

After the game, once we'd shaken hands with the Bowl-O-Rama Llamas, we sat in the dugout in stunned silence as Coach Tom, Coach Joe, and Dad talked about our awesome teamwork and what our strategy would be for the next day's game.

They dismissed us and went to talk to the umpire. No one moved. I kept thinking about Ben's unbelievable home run.

I heard my name and turned to find George grinning at me. "What did you say?" I asked.

George grinned even wider. "Thanks for getting us those snacks."

"It was Luna's idea," I said. "The assistant manager at the Salt Shaker."

"That's not what the snack truck driver said," Abhi protested. "He said it was because of you."

"You're the reason we won," said George. "You brought us luck."

Ben furrowed his brow.

"No, no, we won because we worked together, and Garrett got on base, and Ben hit that stratospheric homer," I said.

"Yeah, how'd a dud like you manage that?" asked Garrett.

Ben turned pink but didn't speak.

"Ben's been practicing hard," said Abhi. "*He hath indeed better bettered expectation than you must expect of me to tell you how.*"

"What's that mean?" asked David.

"Ben could become terrible again, like usual?" asked Garrett.

Abhi waved at him dismissively. "No, it means he's stepped up just when we needed it."

"We got good mojo going," said George. "Quick, let's figure out what we did so we can copy it tomorrow and keep it going."

"We all ate snacks from the Salt Shaker," said Campbell. "That's what must have done it. Those Sports Crisps really work! Next time, I'm trying the truffle fries, too."

"Trish, can you set us up again? Here, take some money. They can't be free forever." George dug in his pocket and pulled out a crumpled five-dollar bill. "Come on, everyone, pay up!"

I shook my head. "I really don't think—"

"Here," said David gruffly, handing me a twenty. "That should be good for a few games."

And with that, almost everyone handed me money.

"What about you, Benny?" Garrett sneered.

Ben shook his head. "I don't need those chips to play well," he said.

"Well, you better get some, because if you bring us bad luck, you'll drag us all down with you."

"He just hit a walk-off home run!" Abhi cried.

"Fluke," said Garrett. "You may have won us this game, but in terms you can understand, your batting average is still like .050."

"It wasn't a fluke!" said Abhi, moving closer to Garrett.

Everyone started talking at once. Ben clenched his jaw but said nothing.

"Okay, okay, enough, guys," said George. "What else did we do today? We have to replicate it exactly tomorrow."

"Ben sat on the left edge of the bench, and I was next to him, and Trish sat next to me," Abhi said. "Garrett and Mike sat at the far end of the bench, all the other guys were in between."

"I wore my lucky bandanna," said Campbell, pointing to a rainbow-striped piece of cloth tied around his neck.

"Well, I'm wearing my lucky socks to every game from now

on," said George. "I won't even wash them. To keep our good luck going."

"I wore my new batting gloves," said Garrett, showing them off.

Mike bumped fists with him. "Lucky gloves, my man."

Abhi squinted at Ben. "What's that on your wrist, Ben?"

Ben turned a pretty watermelon color. "Nothing," he said.

"Come on, show us," said Abhi. "Oh, cool string bracelet. Where'd you get it?"

Ben mumbled something.

"What?" asked Abhi.

"Trish gave it to me," Ben said quietly.

Abhi turned to me, looking delighted. "You did?"

I wasn't all that excited about everyone knowing that I'd made something for Ben. It was kind of embarrassing for him. And me. At least now Ben knew we both wanted to be friends. I held up my own wrist. "I made them. Your sisters showed me a new pattern."

"Double good luck!" Abhi clasped his hands and beamed at me. "And you two played the best today by far! Can I have one? I'd love to pitch like you did. And I wouldn't mind smacking a home run like Ben."

"But—" The bracelet had nothing to do with my pitching or Ben's hit. All our hours of practice did. Although I wasn't sure how much Ben practiced.

"I want one, too," said Mike.

We all turned to him in surprise.

"I want to pitch a no-hitter someday," he said, kicking at the dirt.

Everyone burst out laughing.

"Can you make one for me?" asked Campbell. "They look kind of cool."

In the end, everyone asked for a bracelet, even Garrett.

Show a sign. Following the puzzle book's advice had gotten me more friends in a single afternoon than I'd managed through weeks of struggling. And for once, Ben was looking me in the eye.

Coach Tom came in carrying the equipment bag. "How about we all go get pizza? We have a lot to celebrate today."

And that's how our whole team ended up crowded around a table at Pizza Napoli that night, making a glorious racket. Guys who had barely said two words to me before now chatted with me like I was one of their best friends. Ben laughed, and the sparkle in his eyes reminded me of how he'd been at the Math Puzzler tournament, how quick and confident and brilliant. My heart swelled like it might carry me through the roof and away into the sky.

We demolished the pizza and then went to get ice cream at the Camden Farms stand.

It turned out that Luna was right, after all. The key to

peoples' hearts was through their stomachs. And Aadya and Asha were right, too. String bracelets were a great way to show someone you care.

As we made our way to our cars to go home, Ben came up to me, and my heart did a peculiar little jog.

"Hey Trish," Ben said. "I figured out that problem of yours."

"Oh, yeah?"

He took out the scrap of paper.

1 11 21 1211 111221 312211

"It's not a math problem, right? You just have to say the numbers out loud. You start with one. Then you write how you say it: one one. Then you write how you say that: two ones. And then one two, one one. And on and on . . ."

He had figured it out! "So what's next?" I asked.

"One three, one one, two twos, two ones." Ben turned the paper over and showed me his solution: 13112221.

"Impressive," I said.

"Here's one for you," said Ben. He closed his eyes and recited,

In times or division, it's always the same.
Unus and ein, as victors proclaim.
The lonely, the only, the solo, the sun.
The foxglove, the skullcap, the answer is ___.

"Say it again, slowly," I said.

Ben repeated the poem, and I closed my eyes to listen.

"It's . . . it's *one*, right?" I said.

"One what?" Ben looked confused. Why was he confused?

"The answer. To your puzzle?"

Ben blinked. "Explain why."

"Well, if you multiply by one, or divide by one, you get the same number. That's the first clue. *Ein* means 'one' in German, and *unus* sounds like it's Latin or something. And victors, or winners, say, 'We're number one!' Lonely, only, and solo all imply one, and there's only one sun in the sky. And I don't know about the creepy clothing at the end, but the first two lines rhyme, so I thought the second two lines should rhyme, too. And *one* rhymes with *sun*." I hoped I'd gotten it right. I didn't want to mess up our friendship just as it began. And this just confirmed that Ben was the one who had sent me the book. I had no idea he could write math puzzle poems!

Ben's eyes grew wide. "R-right," he said. "Good job."

I smiled. "That was awesome. Okay, now I have one for you. '*Sixteen great men, all alike. Side by side, we are a foot. But face to face, we are an inch. What are we?*'"

Ben scowled. "How is that a math problem?"

"It's a math *puzzle*," I said. "If you can't figure it out, you should look in your pocket."

"What's that supposed to mean?" asked Ben.

"You'll see," I said. "And Ben, that was such an amazing hit. How'd it feel to—"

But he was already on his way back to his car.

Abhi came up to me and bumped fists. “What do you think, Trish? Maybe now our luck has changed for good?”

“I don’t believe in luck,” I said.

But I just might believe in that weird math book. Following its advice had not only helped me make friends with Ben, it helped me make friends with the whole team. Now I needed to figure out the answer to the next puzzle.

Chapter Twelve

Ben

The Second Puzzle

As soon as I got home, I ran to my bedroom, grabbed *The Mathematics of The Wild*, and wrote the answer: *1*.

Sure enough, it turned bright green. I would have figured it out eventually, but Trish's help got me there much faster.

Underneath the green *1*, a sentence appeared: *Show you care.*

What did that mean? Show the baseball I cared about it? Or show *Trish*? That was a terrifying idea. But it was a small price to pay for more hits and another game won.

I turned the page eagerly, hoping for another fun math puzzle, but what I found completely baffled me. It wasn't even another poem.

It was a drawing of a series of leaves and a seed:

I scratched my head and tried to swap things around to see whether a pattern emerged:

But that didn't get me anywhere. The leaves were smooth and oval, and didn't have any sections, so there were no numbers obviously associated with them. And what did that seed mean? Maybe they stood for numbers, and I had to add arithmetic symbols so they made an equation?

It was maddening. I stared at the page for over an hour with no ideas until Fib put his head in my lap to tell me it was time for bed.

I wondered if Trish would have any ideas. But I couldn't ask her unless I knew the answer to the puzzle she'd given me, and I had no clue how to solve it.

I curled up to visions of leaves and seeds whirling in my head and finally fell into a fitful sleep.

The next morning, I started reading a new Fibonacci biography over my bowl of cereal. I'd already read a lot about Fibonacci numbers, but it was cool to think about the man himself, coming up with number theories on his own in twelfth-century Italy. Then Fib trotted into the room, followed by Dad.

"That was quite a hit yesterday, Ben. I can see you've been working on squaring up and putting your legs into it. I saw how you brought your hip around."

I looked up briefly. I knew that home run had to do with the magic math book and not any tips Dad had given me. "Guess so," I said, and then went back to my book.

"Does this mean—do you think—are you going to play ball in the spring? Because, if you are, I'll sign up to coach."

I looked up again and sighed. "I'm not sure, Dad. Whether playing in the spring is a good idea."

"But after that home run—"

"It was just one game. I'll probably be back to terrible today." I hid behind the book again.

"Ben, we should talk," said Dad.

"Don't need to." I certainly didn't want to.

"I'd love for you to keep playing. And Grandma Beth wouldn't want you to quit," Dad said quietly. "She loved baseball, and she loved playing with you. Her Fountain of Youth, she called it."

That was totally unfair, bringing Grandma into it. There

was Dad, putting pressure on me again. I put down my book and took a deep breath. "I think she'd say I should listen to my instincts."

I went back to reading, hoping he wouldn't say anything else. After a minute or two of silence, Dad left the room. Fib whimpered and curled up at my feet.

I bit the inside of my mouth. I was glad Dad hadn't made me say it out loud.

Dad shouldn't be a head coach. Never again. He'd already made enough coaching mistakes for a lifetime.

Later that day, the stomach butterflies were in full force as I arrived at the field for our away game against the Banbury Bakery Buns. Like Garrett had said, my hit from the day before probably had been a fluke. But I kept thinking about the book's advice, just the same.

Trish arrived at the game with Sports Crisps for everyone. She returned everyone's money, too; it turned out the chips were five dollars a pop, but the store manager wanted to keep giving them to us for free because we were the Salt Shaker's sponsored team. And I guess because she liked Trish, or maybe because Trish was great at convincing her.

Was it possible the chips made us play better? Of course the Salt Shaker wouldn't put stuff in them that actually made people play better, but maybe they had brought us luck? I figured it was worth it to cover all possibilities. Besides, they were delicious.

Trish had also managed to make a bracelet for every player on the team. Was this her way of showing the whole team that she *cared*? For some reason, that annoyed me. But I spun the string bracelet on my wrist and hoped it brought me luck again.

Dad and Coach Deepak laid out the batting helmets and posted the lineup. My jaw dropped when I saw the list.

"We have you batting cleanup after yesterday's mega hit," Dad said, clapping me on the back. "Remember, keep your bat level and you'll continue to do well." I plastered on a smile but groaned inside. When I sat next to Abhi on the bench, I couldn't help grumbling to him. "Why's my dad always trying to make me seem like I'm way better than I am?"

"I wish my dad would do that," Abhi said, slumping in his seat. "My dad only focuses on my math skills instead of baseball skills. This doesn't count to him. I wish he at least came to some of my games."

Of course, Abhi was right. I shouldn't have complained about my dad when Abhi was still waiting for his to notice him. I tried to distract him by flipping my lucky coin. "Look at that. Four heads in a row," I said.

"Excellent," Abhi said with a grin. "*O Fate! Take not away thy heavy hand!*"

We jogged onto the field to warm up.

During the game, I followed the book's advice and tried telling the ball I cared about it while I was fielding. Sure, it was ridiculous. But I held my glove over my mouth so no one could see my lips move and whispered so no one could hear me. And I didn't drop a single ball, despite having to catch a tricky little pop-up while staring into the sun.

The whole team played better—David pitched well, and we scored enough to keep the game within reach. George was faster than ever, and Abhi wrecked a double. I went 2 for 3 with an RBI. I overheard Coach Tom tell Dad he was glad all my practice was finally paying off.

But when I sat on the bench, the two math puzzles I was supposed to solve gnawed at my mind. Trish's puzzle involved men who were "all alike," and feet, and inches. But that seemed better than trying to comprehend what leaves and seeds had to do with math. I gave Trish a wide berth and tried not to look at her, just in case she asked about her puzzle. I didn't want to talk to her about it until I'd solved it.

We were tied 4–4 when we got up to bat at the top of the sixth inning. I flipped the coin out of habit.

It came up heads five more times.

"That's impossible," I said. "Nine times in a row?"

"It's a trick coin," said Garrett.

"Nope," said Abhi.

"But the odds of that happening are really small, right?" asked George.

"Yes, it's—" I scrambled to calculate 0.5 times 9 . . .

"Point two percent," Trish said.

I flipped again. Heads.

"What were the chances of that?" asked Abhi.

"Point zero one percent," I said with a dry mouth.

I flipped the coin again, but Garrett knocked it out of the air before I could catch it.

"What'd you do that for?" I asked.

"You're creeping everyone out, man," said Garrett.

"I think it's kind of cool," said George.

The coin had rolled under the bench near me, and I crawled under it and reached around. As my fingers closed around its warm metal, something clicked in my head.

I knew the answer to Trish's puzzle. But I needed to get home to make sure.

First, though, I got up to bat and smacked a triple down the right field line.

We ended up beating the Banbury Bakery Buns 10–4.

Chapter Thirteen

Trish
The Most Important Heart

I sat at the kitchen counter crouched over *The Mathematics of The Wild*. The next puzzle appeared weirdly personal:

Though you would fain to be reclusive
In this summer of your discontent,
From 1 to 1,000 inclusive,
What digit is the most frequent?

Did Ben make this up? It was a poem, which was like the math puzzle he shared with me after our first win, so it was possible. But this language sounded more like something Abhi would have written.

I thought about the puzzle. I didn't know what fain meant, but I had been like a recluse for most of the summer, even while sitting in the dugout. I'd been the odd man out . . .

since I wasn't a man. Until the game we finally won, there had been an invisible barrier between me and everyone else. And I'd certainly felt plenty of discontent. As for the actual math question, I was pretty sure I knew the answer. It had to do with the fact that one thousand was included . . .

"Hi, sweetie," Mom said, walking into the kitchen. "I hear your baseball season has taken a turn for the better."

I was excited and a little flustered to hear Mom talking about baseball. I closed the book and hid it under a stack of magazines. I wanted to keep it secret for now since I didn't want to open up a conversation about the Math Puzzler team.

I nodded. "Our pitching's always been great, but now everyone's hitting well, and we're working better together as a team."

"That's wonderful. I hope to come to a game this weekend. Oh, and I'm going to ask the league about getting AEDs at each field."

"What's an AED?"

"Come help me with dinner, and I'll explain."

"Okay." I got up and washed my hands.

"I prepped everything already. Can you make the cauliflower curry while I get the rice started?"

"Sure." Mom had already laid the ingredients out. I heated a pan on the stove, then added some oil, cumin seeds, black mustard seeds, and a pinch of turmeric. I covered the pan and turned down the heat. Once the seeds had finished popping, I added chopped onion. I inhaled the pungent aromas and enjoyed the music of the onions sizzling. After a few minutes, I stirred in tomato paste, cooked it for half a minute, then added our favorite curry powder, toasting it for a few seconds before I added cauliflower florets, chopped tomatoes, and some water. I stirred everything together, coating the cauliflower in the spices, then sprinkled in some salt and water, covered the pot, and increased the heat again so everything would steam.

"An AED is an automated external defibrillator. An AED can zap a person's heart if it stops beating due to an abnormal rhythm."

I shook my head. Mom was always scoping out potential heart attacks: large guys sweating in restaurants, women clutching their stomachs at parties. "Why would someone's heart stop at a baseball game?"

"You never know," Mom said seriously. "It could happen to an umpire or one of the spectators, or even a player if they get thumped in the chest in just the wrong way."

I shrugged. I'd gotten hit in the chest a few times, and nothing had happened to me. But Mom was a cardiologist, so she saw heart problems everywhere.

Mom put a container of cooked chickpeas on the counter for me. She carefully lifted the pot of cooked brown rice out of the pressure cooker and set it aside to cool.

"Are you making cumin rice?" I asked.

She smiled. "Yes. Hand me those cumin seeds, please." She heated oil in a pan and toasted the seeds until they were dark and fragrant.

"Did you get the good yogurt?" I asked.

"Yes, darling," said Mom.

I chuckled as I checked on the curry and gave it a stir. I closed the lid again as Mom finished making the cumin rice.

"Thanks for taking care of that," said Mom. "I already made the cucumber and tomato salad."

It was so good to be cooking with Mom again. We hadn't done this since we'd moved, and I missed it.

"Mom," I said. "Can I talk to you about something?"

She turned to me and wiped her hands on a dishcloth. "Of course. Are you okay?"

I nodded. It was time. If I could talk to Mom about the Math Puzzler tournament, maybe she'd help me figure out a way to tell Ben. I took a deep breath. "It's about the—"

Mom's beeper went off. She spent a few moments reading it, then went to the sink and washed her hands. A worry line had appeared between her eyes. "Sorry, honey, I've got to go in. Please let Dad and Sanjay know, okay?"

"What is it?" I asked.

"It's an acute MI. A heart attack. We've got to get that artery open ASAP. That's the most important thing to do to save this patient's heart." Mom had already grabbed her hospital badge and was halfway to the garage door.

I was sorry that someone was having a heart attack. But there were other doctors. Why did Mom always have to be the one they called? Why couldn't we just have a meal together like normal people?

I set the table and finished bringing the serving dishes out just as Dad and Sanjay followed the scent of the food into the kitchen.

"Where's Mom?" asked Sanjay.

I gritted my teeth. "One guess."

"Cath lab, huh?" Dad asked.

I nodded. "We never get to eat together anymore." Against my will, my lip started to quiver.

Dad patted my back. "We all miss her. Once she gets everything set up, it will get better. It won't be this way forever."

"She's saving lives, Trish," said Sanjay, serving himself some rice.

I took a few bites of dinner, but it tasted flavorless.

I wondered what it would feel like if *my* heart were the most important thing in Mom's life.

After dinner I wanted to distract myself, so I went to my room and thought about the puzzle again. The digits 1 to 9 occurred with the same frequency every ten numbers, and 0 occurred less frequently because there were no double zero digits like 11, 22, etc. But if you included 1000, the answer was clear: the number that occurred the most frequently was 1.

I wrote it in the book, and the number turned green. What kind of cool science made it do that? Then the invisible ink sentence became visible:

Make it fun.

Easier said than done.

I turned the page and found another puzzle.

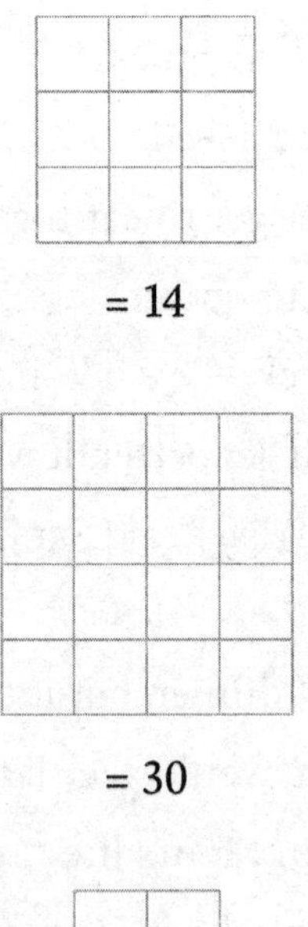

= ?

I stared at it for a while and jotted down some notes, but the numbers started to get ugly.

It was clear this would take more thought.

I stopped by the Salt Shaker again before practice on Thursday. After waiting in line for twenty minutes, I ordered some Sports Crisps and lemonade and asked Ivy whether Luna was in.

"Of course she is, my lovely favored dear. I'll go and fetch her, worry not—wait here."

I stood in the corner until Luna hopped over the counter and greeted me. "Trish! How wonderful to see you! Do you need more supplies for the team? The snack truck is usually out for deliveries in other towns, but you can drop by here before your games to pick up whatever you need."

"No," I said. "I just wondered whether you had a few minutes to talk."

"Of course," said Luna. "Come back here to the office."

Luna opened a half door for me so I didn't need to jump the counter, and I followed her behind the counter. Salt Shaker employees gave me nods or smiles as I passed, while the other customers stared in amazement tinged with jealousy at the special treatment I was getting. We made our way into a tiny office off the kitchen. It was painted an electric green, and contained a large wooden desk, curiously carved and covered in papers. Hanging above it was a calendar filled with notes for each day, as well as some sort of timetable for organizing the Salt Shaker kitchen. There was also a framed quote, decorated with leaves and flowers: *To business that we love we rise betimes, and go to't with delight.* I smiled; it seemed like something Abhi would say.

Luna motioned me toward the chair at the empty desk, then sat. "How can I help you, Trish?"

Now that I was here, I was embarrassed to talk. Why *was* I here?

"Have you made friends on the team now? After the snacks?"

"Oh, yes. And it's so generous of you to give them to us for free. But . . ." It would be awkward to complain to Luna—who was clearly a strong, popular leader—that now that Ben was talking to me, I didn't know how to confess my secret and have him not hate me. *Remember that math tournament where I humiliated you?*

"Yes?" Luna raised her eyebrows.

"I need to talk to someone about something I did. Well, I *didn't* do it, but everyone thinks I did. But it was a mistake. But not my mistake, their mistake. I'm not explaining this well . . ."

"Hmm," said Luna, tilting her head. "It's hard to keep a secret. It's also hard to reveal one. Eventually, though, it's likely to come out, so it's better if you do the telling." Her cheeks

flushed, and her yellow-green eyes sparkled.

My shoulders slumped. "You're right. But I don't know how to begin, or even how to get him alone so I can tell him without telling the whole world at the same time."

"Perhaps you could get him in a good mood, and then tell him?"

"Maybe. But how?"

Luna started pacing the tiny room. "Maybe do something to make him look good in front of the rest of the team?"

I thought about it for a moment, and the beginning of an idea sprouted in my mind. "I think I could do that."

A knock disturbed us, and Ivy poked his head into the office. "There seems to be a problem with the spice blend," he said. "Our worries in this town, they never end!"

Luna lifted her chin. "Can't Rob take care of this? Where is he?"

Ivy shook his head. "Master Robin's nowhere to be found. Thank goodness that we have your smarts around."

"One moment, please, Ivy." Luna turned to me. "Anything else you need, Trish?"

I stood. "You've helped me so much. Sorry for interrupting your day. Our next game is a home game on Saturday at one, so I'll be here at eleven thirty."

"Excellent," said Luna. "Follow me, and I'll show you the back entrance to the kitchen. That way, you can pick up your orders before away games, too, and you won't need to wait in line and risk being late."

I grabbed Luna's arm and squeezed. She was so kind. "Thank you so much. You know, the whole team believes that . . . that your snacks make us play better."

"That's the idea," Luna said with a smile.

"But—I'm just checking—there's not actually anything *in* the snacks that would . . . you know, make us *actually* play better, right?" I had to ask. I hated shortcuts and detested cheating.

Luna inspected me with her startling yellow eyes. "Of course not, Trish. They're just tasty. No need to feel guilty about eating them. Although I can't help what superstitions build up around our snacks. There are many teams who think we've improved their luck."

Hmm. I knew there was no such thing as luck, but I couldn't fight my whole team's baseball superstitions now that we were winning.

We walked through the tiny kitchen where green- and blue-shirted employees worked in a coordinated rhythm that once again reminded me of a dance. "Attention, everyone." Luna clapped her hands. "This is Trish, the rising star of the Salt Shaker baseball team." Six pairs of different colored eyes turned to stare at me. "She'll be coming to this back entrance at least once a week, maybe more, with a special order. Please fill it as quickly as possible. The one who gets Trish's order to her the fastest wins a prize," she said with a smile.

The other employees nodded at me and grinned.

"Luna," said Ivy. "We—"

"Coming, Ivy," said Luna. She turned to me. "Until Saturday, then, Trish."

"Thanks," I said.

As I made my way down the sidewalk to Bailey Park, my idea came together.

I knew a way to show Ben how much we had in common and make him look good in front of the rest of the team. I wanted to play a game that Ben would get, and win.

And I'd be sure to *make it fun*.

Chapter Fourteen

Ben

This Is a Stick

Dad had to work and couldn't come to the next practice, so I took Fib with me. He trotted at my side as I made my way through the woods. Halfway to the field, Fib started whining and sprinted off the path into the trees. I tried to follow him, but he had completely disappeared.

"Fib!" I was happy he could run again, but this wandering off had to stop.

"Ben? Is that you?" came a familiar voice.

I ran back to the path, where Rob stood with his arms crossed and a preoccupied smile on his face. "Are you lost?" he asked.

I laughed and wished I could run into Rob on the baseball field for once, where he could actually teach me something. "No, just chasing after my dog again."

"How fortunate that I'm seeing you. I have great news." His blond hair shined almost as brightly as his sparkly baseball cap, and his eyes glinted.

"What news?"

"Well, it pertains to a star player like you," said Rob.

Whoa! I couldn't believe that the best baseball player I'd met in person was calling me a star! "I've been having a hitting streak, it's true."

"Come now, Ben. I've been watching your games and talking to people around town. You are responsible for your team's success! And we at the Salt Shaker have concocted a plan to make sure that the best players get extra-special treatment."

"What do you—"

"The Salt Shaker has arranged it so the winning team of each age division will get to attend a Turkeys game in August and meet the entire team."

"What? That's incredible!"

"You'd better try your hardest, then, right, Ben? And hope for a bit of luck." Rob gave me a wink.

"I am trying my hardest," I said. "And my lucky coin's been saying that our team would win."

"What do you mean, lucky coin?" Rob asked.

"It was my grandmother's. It helps predict the outcomes of games," I said. "Heads we win, tails we lose. And last game it came up heads ten times in a row."

"How about that?" Rob said with a curious expression. "That's rather improbable, isn't it? Say . . . have you come across any other interesting math problems lately?"

I knew it! "Well, I—"

"Hello, Robin. Hello, young man." Rob's silver-haired friend glided up to us. "How are you this lovely summer day?" His voice was creaky and whispery, like a tree bending in the wind, and it sent a chill down my spine.

Rob's face closed up. I knew what that meant.

He had a secret.

"Hello," I said. "I'm Ben."

"Mr. O," said the silver-haired man, shaking my hand. "Owner of the Salt Shaker."

"Oh, wow, thank you. The free snacks for our baseball team have been awesome."

Mr. O raised a silver eyebrow. "Free snacks?"

I nodded warily. Didn't the owner know? "We're the Salt Shaker's sponsored baseball team. Your manager's been sending us snacks, and we've been winning ever since. It's got everyone in town talking about your store."

Mr. O patted Rob's shoulder. "You have been hard at work, I see."

Rob nodded but didn't say anything. Didn't Trish say it was a *female* manager who had been giving us the snacks?

"Well, congratulations, my dear boy. All the best to you

and our Salt Shaker team. And you"—Mr. O fixed Rob with a piercing look—"how is our summer project going? Are we . . . still ahead, despite your . . . generosity? *Are you working well with your partner?* You are not wasting time playing again, are you, dear Robin?"

"No, my—uncle." Rob glanced at me, then ducked his head and stared at the ground. "Everything is going splendidly."

"Make sure it is done, and done correctly," said Mr. O. "Everything depends upon this summer, as you very well know."

Rob nodded, still not looking at Mr. O. "Fear not, my lord, your servant shall do so. I am forever faithful," he said.

What were they talking about? It sounded like Abhi had written their conversation for them, dug up from some musty old Shakespeare play.

Mr. O clapped Rob on the shoulder. "My right-hand man, as always." He turned to me. "Farewell, young man. I will come and observe your team again soon." Then he turned and walked away, disappearing into the woods in a few moments.

Observe? He made it sound like we were zoo specimens. "What was that about?" I asked Rob. "He's your uncle?"

"Yes," said Rob. "But mainly, he's my boss. Like he said, no ball games for me." And he took off on the path toward town without saying another word.

I sighed. It really was too bad Rob couldn't play ball—he obviously loved it so much. I found myself wishing that Rob's uncle and Abhi's dad would both let the boys they loved play the game they loved with no guilt.

Just as I mentally prepared myself for another search in the woods for Fib, I heard the jingle of a collar. Fib trotted to me and presented his belly for me to scratch, showing that his entire furry body was covered in green dust.

"Yeah, you'd better be sorry," I said sternly. "It's not nice to stay hidden when a friend's calling your name. Come on, get up."

Fib sat and panted in my face as I clipped on his leash. "You'd think you're related to Rob or something, with the way you disappear and reappear so quickly."

Fib wagged the rest of the way to Bailey Park.

I had an amazing practice, smacking hits right and left and even making a spectacular diving catch in the outfield. I *was* becoming the star of the team, way better than annoying Garrett, better than David and Abhi. Maybe even better than Trish. And if I got to meet the Turkeys, it would make my year. Possibly my decade.

"I know the answer to your puzzle," I said to Trish as we were packing up.

"Yeah?" she asked, adjusting the cap on her head.

I tossed her a penny.

She caught it and grinned. "I knew you'd get it."

"It was kind of cool. I tried quarters, nickels, and dimes first, but these were the ones that stacked up to an inch and measured a foot when I put them side by side. Your clue about my pocket kind of gave it away."

Trish giggled. "Glad it made you think. Great shirt, by the way."

I'd forgotten about it. I had the binary numbers shirt on again. I laughed. "Thanks."

"Want to play a game?" Trish asked.

"What kind of game?"

"The kind we're good at," she said with twinkling eyes. "Hey guys, listen up," she called to the rest of the team, who gathered around.

Trish held up a stick. "So, this is a stick." She pointed to a bat and her backpack. "This is a stick, and this is a stick." She took off her baseball cap and showed it to me. "Is this a stick?"

What was this stupidity? "No," I said.

"Yes, it is," said Trish, grinning.

I scowled.

"Let me do it again," said Trish. She pointed at the equipment bag. "This is a stick." She pointed at the bench, then a batting helmet. "This is a stick, and this is a stick." She held up a stick. "Is this a stick?"

"Yes?" I asked, hating the question in my voice. Of course it was!

"No, it's not," said Trish. She smiled like she was the smartest kid in the world, and I was her poor slow cousin. "Let me give you more examples. So, this is a stick, and this is a stick, and this is a stick," she said, pointing at a pair of sunglasses, David's catcher's mitt, and a water bottle. "Is this a stick?" She pointed at Abhi.

"No," I said. Surely people couldn't be sticks?

"*Yes*," said Trish, staring at me and tilting her head like we were sharing some sort of secret.

She was making fun of me! Just when I thought we were friends. What the heck?

"Let me try," said Abhi.

"Okay," said Trish. "This is a stick and this is a stick and this is a stick," she said, pointing to her cleat, home plate, and Garrett's nose. "Is this a stick?" She pointed at her bat.

"No," said Abhi with a grin.

"Right! So, if this is a stick, and this is a stick, and this is a stick," she pointed at her water bottle, the dugout fence, and my lucky coin. "Is this a stick?" She pointed at Fib.

"Yes!" said Abhi.

"Right!" said Trish. They both dissolved into laughter.

It was maddening.

They kept going. Now that Abhi had figured out Trish's dumb game, he started asking questions, too. Then George got it. Then Campbell. Then Garrett. "It's so easy, Ben," he said. "Don't you get it? There are two kinds of people: Those who get puzzles, and those who don't." He glanced at my shirt and snickered.

My face heated up. I stared at the dirt. Garrett was right. I didn't understand the joke, and it was driving me batty. The rest of the team was cracking up with laughter, but a dull headache throbbed behind my eyes.

"Maybe we should stop," Trish said. She lowered her voice. "Should I tell you the trick?"

"No," I said shortly. I didn't need her charity. "I should get home." Trish had set me up. She'd fooled Abhi. She'd pretended to be my friend, made me put my guard down, and then punched me right in the gut.

"You're the best, Trish," said Garrett. "You've turned a team of total losers into winners. *And* you're the smartest kid in town."

I hurried to finish packing up and stalked away. How was *Trish* getting all the credit for our team's amazing turnaround?

"Ben," Trish said, but I ignored her and called Fib to me to head home. In my hurry, I stepped in a hole in the sod and fell, twisting my foot. It hurt worse than my bruised feelings. When I finally struggled to my feet, listening for the sound of my team's laughter, I found Abhi standing next to me.

"Dude, there was a trick," he said. "If she started her

statements with 'so,' it meant that whatever she pointed to at the end was a stick. If she didn't start with 'so,' it wasn't."

"Great. Thanks for confirming that I'm the stupidest kid on the team," I said. My ankle throbbed. Had I hurt it enough to affect my baseball playing? How much worse could this day get?

"Ben, don't—"

I hauled on Fib's leash and hobbled into the woods.

I couldn't figure out the next puzzle in the math book. That's why Trish was succeeding in making my best friend care more about her than me. And if I didn't solve the puzzle, would my baseball playing get worse, and would the team start losing again?

This was what it meant to be the only, the lonely, the solo, the one.

I hobbled a bit farther down the path, slipped Trish's bracelet off my wrist, and flung it into the brush around me. I kept moving, but my ankle was killing me. Eventually, I sat down to take off my shoe and look at how bad it was.

"I did a great job on myself, huh, Fib?"

My ankle was swollen like an overripe piece of fruit and touching it anywhere was excruciating. Just when my baseball career was taking off, this had to happen.

Fib whined and kissed my ankle with a green-dust-covered muzzle, and the throbbing eased.

"Thanks, boy. Let's get home."

It was only when I finally limped into my yard that I realized what the answer to the magical math book's puzzle was.

And Trish was the reason I'd figured it out.

Chapter Fifteen

Trish

Intense

I thought Ben would be the first to catch on to the riddle. Instead, he was practically the only one on the team who didn't. How could I have made such a terrible mistake? I packed up quickly and joined Dad, who was waiting to walk home with me.

"It's great to see you laughing with your teammates," said Dad.

I shrugged.

"What's the matter?" asked Dad.

"Nothing." I didn't want to tell him about how badly I'd misjudged things. Just when Ben and I were starting to become friends, I'd messed everything up.

"Want to stop by that snack shop on the way home?" Dad asked. "Everyone in town's been talking about their chips and fries."

"No thanks. I eat too much of their stuff already. We have their snacks at every game, remember?"

"I want to check out their full menu. Let's go see if their lines are as long as people say."

Sure enough, the line at the Salt Shaker was the longest I'd ever seen it. In the window, a bright blue poster caught my attention, and I scanned it quickly.

"Dad, look! The winning teams in our league will get to meet the Turkeys!" I said.

"Our team's in the running," Dad said.

I nodded. "It's possible, but it'll be challenging. We need to win the rest of our regular season games and hope not to face the Camemberts until the championship game of the tournament. And even then, it will be tough."

"Yep," said Dad. "But a chance to meet the Turkeys gives us all an extra incentive."

If we somehow won the tournament, would Ben find a way to forgive me? Could we go back to cooperating instead of competing?

We walked a few minutes in silence when something occurred to me. "Dad," I said. "If I weren't good at math, would you be upset?"

"Where is this coming from?"

"Well, my friend Abhi is an amazing ballplayer, and he's memorized like all the works of Shakespeare, but his dad doesn't care about anything but his math scores. He's kind of obsessed."

Dad rubbed his chin. "I can understand. That's how your grandfather felt about me."

I was so shocked I stopped walking. "He did? But he's so proud of you! And he's so chill."

"He's proud now. And much more chill." Dad laughed. "But he fought me tooth and nail when I said I wanted to be a graphic designer. He thought I'd be starving and homeless."

"But why?"

"He was allowed to immigrate to the U.S. because he was an engineer. Same with most of the other Indians he knew, who only got immigration visas because they worked in technology or medicine. He was afraid that if I didn't stick with a technical or scientific field, I'd never get a job."

"But you did get a job. You make awesome art. And you're your own boss." Thank goodness, I thought, because with Mom always at the hospital or the lab, I was glad to have one parent who could go to school events.

"It all worked out," said Dad. "But now that I'm an adult, I understand why my dad was so concerned. He only knew what worked for him, and he was scared that if I strayed from that path, it might turn into a disaster."

I chewed on my lip. No matter how much Abhi's dad was looking toward the future, shaming him now wouldn't help anything. "Did Mom's parents put pressure on her to be a doctor?"

Dad laughed. "They didn't need to. She's wanted to go into medicine since forever. When we became friends in college, she was the most intense person I'd ever met."

Mom did everything like she was being graded on it. "She still is."

Dad put his arm around my shoulder. "You know, she reminds me of someone."

I pushed his arm away and strode faster. I wasn't like Mom. I refused to be.

Mom spent all her time working toward her goals. Well, so did I, but that was only because circumstances made me have to. If I wasn't the best, I wouldn't even be on the teams I loved so much. And I never let baseball or math get in the way of being with my family, but Mom found a way to always be working and never with us.

We approached a bakery called the While Away Café, which was also quite busy. "Oh, I've been wanting to come here for weeks. Let's stop in and pick up something," said Dad.

"I don't want dessert." But at his disappointed look, I told him I'd hang outside while he bought what he wanted.

What I wanted to do was think. About if I really was like Mom, whether I could help Abhi with his dad, and how I could possibly fix things with Ben. I leaned against the brick of the building and closed my eyes for a moment.

"Stop worrying!" came a harsh whisper. "It's going to work out."

I looked around, but all I could see were two long shadows on the pavement of the parking lot behind the café.

"But my book is missing, and now you tell me yours is, too? Doesn't that sound like foul play?" said another voice.

I crept along the wall toward the voices. At least one seemed familiar, but it was hard to tell from just whispers.

"You seem to be doing just fine," said the first voice.

"Mistakes are being made, and not because of me. You only think everything's fine because you're not paying attention!"

"I've got an important project," said the first voice.

"You're supposed to be helping *me*. Us. You know what's at stake," hissed the second voice. "You know the penalty."

"I said it was *important*," said the first voice. "It involves important people."

"I need you to pay attention to *our* people! There are strange things afoot."

"Don't you just follow the instructions?"

"There are nuances that must be accounted for, which you'd know if you ever came around to work."

"You've made it clear you don't need me mucking about."

"I don't want you mucking about! I want you to help. If we lose the wager . . ."

"Ah, yes. The wager, always the wager," said the first voice.

"That's how it's been for eternity. Worry not."

"We were charged to work *together*."

"I said don't tell me what to do!"

I moved a few steps closer. In another couple feet, I might just be able to lean over and see who was talking.

"I got an incredible assortment of cupcakes, including a couple that taste like gulab jamun," came Dad's voice from behind me. "Trish? Where are you?"

I held my breath and hoped the voices would continue talking, but they hushed, and the shadows grew longer and then faded away.

"Trish?"

"Coming, Dad," I said.

I didn't say much on the rest of the short walk home. I wondered about the whispered conversation I overheard, and what it meant.

Most of it made no sense. There was something in it that seemed familiar, but I couldn't remember what, or where, or when. And I had the strangest feeling that it had to do with me.

Mom wasn't home for dinner again, so Dad set aside some lasagna for her, then Sanjay, Dad, and I had cupcakes from the bakery. I took a bite of Dad's gulab jamun cupcake, which tasted remarkably like the dessert. But sweets aren't my thing. Part of me longed for a taste of Sports Crisps or truffle fries so I could remember what it was like to be happy on my baseball team. Maybe I could use the Morale-Boosting Mint Crackers to make myself feel better about Ben? I sighed and took my plate to the dishwasher.

Sanjay threw me a concerned look, but I did my best to avoid his eyes.

"I'm going up to my room," I said.

I lay on my bed and tried to focus on my book about the All-American Girls Professional Baseball League, when women played ball while all the male players were off fighting in World War II. What an incredible time that must have been! There was a knock at my door, and Sanjay poked his head in. "Want to talk?"

"Sure." I rolled over on my back and put down the book.

"Spill it," Sanjay said, sitting on the side of my bed.

"It's Ben. Just when I thought we were friends, I had to go and ruin everything."

"Ruin? How?"

I chewed on my lip. "I embarrassed him."

"At practice? But Claudia said he's suddenly gotten amazing at baseball."

I shook my head. "This doesn't have anything to do with baseball. Well, not directly."

Sanjay waited in silence. He knew how to sweat a secret out of me.

"I . . . I played the This Is a Stick game with the team."

Sanjay slapped his leg and started to laugh. "Don't tell me . . . genius Ben didn't get it and got all bent out of shape."

I sat up. "How did you know? It's not funny. He hates me now!"

Sanjay managed to stop laughing, but he couldn't wipe the grin off his face. "Oh, man. I know Ben's great at math, but being book smart doesn't always mean you can think out of the box. Or like a stick."

I sighed. "He was *so mad*! And I was trying to make him look good in front of the team."

"My advice? Don't try to make it up to Ben in public. Just take him aside and apologize."

I nodded. "I'll try."

But the secret I wasn't telling anyone stood between us like a wall higher than the Green Monster in Boston.

Sanjay stood and walked to the door. "I'm taking Claudia to a late movie. See you tomorrow, okay?"

"Good night," I said. "Tell Claudia hi for me."

I didn't feel like reading anymore. I flipped to the math puzzle from *The Mathematics of The Wild*, but I couldn't concentrate. I closed the book with a groan, flopped on my bed, and stared at the Turkeys poster on my wall. How had everything gone so wrong? I needed to somehow step back and see the big picture.

Wait a second . . . the big picture! I grabbed the book and turned to the puzzle page again.

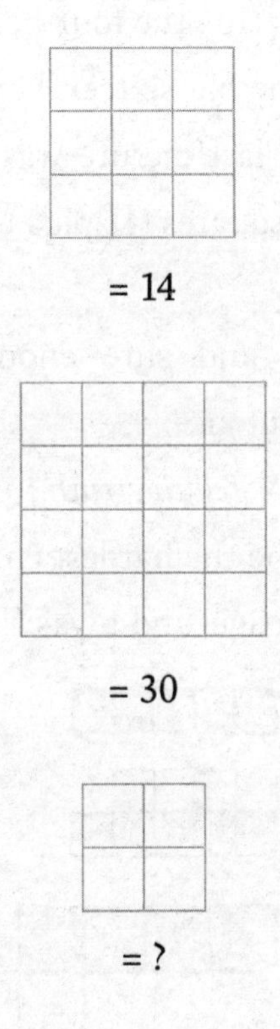

It wasn't about calculating the area of the squares, or calculating anything at all, really. It wasn't about figuring out how to make nine squares equal fourteen, or sixteen squares equal thirty. That resulted in some hideous, non-integer numbers. It was about looking at the big picture.

The numbers described the total number of squares in each picture! In the first picture, this meant all the one-box squares (9), the four-box squares (4), plus the big nine-box square (1)—and 9 + 4 + 1 = 14. In the second picture, the answer included all the one-box squares (16), the four-box squares (9), the nine-box squares (4), plus the big sixteen-box square (1)—and 16 + 9 + 4 + 1 = 30. So the last picture was actually the easiest. I added up the one-box squares (4), plus the big four-box square (1)—and 4 + 1 = 5.

I wrote it down, and sure enough, it turned green. Underneath it was a sentence:

Tell the truth.

That was going to be the hardest challenge of all.

Then I turned the page, and I was floored.

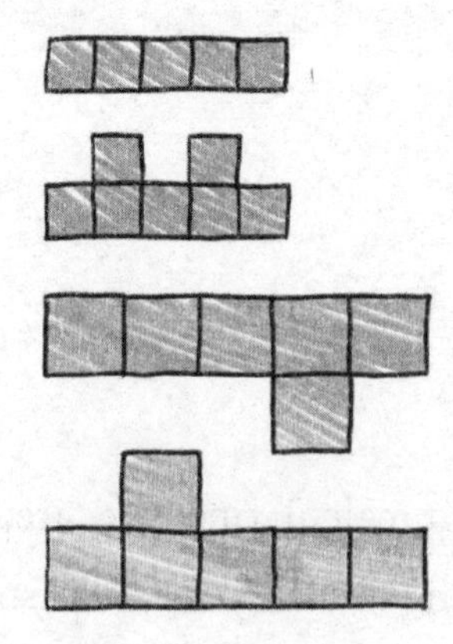

What in the world did that mean?

Chapter Sixteen

Ben

The Ecstasy and the Agony

Things were going great. Fantastic, in fact.

When I got home after the This Is a Stick nightmare, I went back to the puzzle in *The Mathematics of The Wild* again. It turned out that the answer was *on my shirt* the whole time.

The leaves and the seed stood for digits, with the leaves representing ones and the seeds a zero. Like this: 1101. But 1101 isn't particularly special—it's not even prime since it's divisible by three.

But then I thought: There are only ones and zeroes. What if it's in binary?

Like on the shirt I was wearing. The one Trish liked so much.

In binary, you can only use ones and zeroes, but you still can make any decimal number. But instead of the places being the ones, tens, hundreds, thousands, and so on in powers of ten, the places are ones, twos, fours, eights, sixteens, and on and on in powers of two. So:

0 = 0

1 = 1

2 = 10 (like on my T-shirt, *There are 10 kinds of people . . .*)

3 = 11

And in this case, 1101 = one 1, no 2s, one 4, and one 8, which was *13*.

A special number. A *prime* number. I'd cracked the code!

I wrote my answer, and it turned green. Underneath it, a sentence appeared:

Reveal what's in your heart.

Well, after starting off the summer feeling trapped playing baseball, I'd managed to improve my playing enough that I remembered all the things I loved about the game. The thrill of a hit, the satisfaction of a good catch, the feeling that only came from sitting in a dugout with friends. I *had* revealed my heart.

My heart was with my team.

I didn't need to care about Trish. Even if she said she wanted to be friends. She'd humiliated me in front of everyone, so she didn't deserve to be my friend.

She didn't.

I turned the page, and the next puzzle had appeared:

182^ = 13

90^ = 9

30^ = 5

6^ = ?

That was going to take some thought, but I knew I'd get it eventually. I was on a high in baseball and math, and nothing was getting in my way.

Trish came up to me before the start of our next game. "Ben, can we talk? I just want to—"

But I turned away and acted like I didn't hear.

Abhi had seen what happened. "Talk to her," he said. "*How much better is it to weep at joy than to joy at weeping!*"

"I don't see Trish weeping," I said. Though she did look pretty sad. She deserved to.

After eating up the Sports Crisps and truffle fries supplied by the Salt Shaker, we started our game against the Margherita's Pizza Players. Trish's fastball seemed slower than usual, and she let three runs score in the first inning, but I narrowed their lead to one with a two-run triple in the bottom of the first. By the time we got to the bottom of the fourth, we were ahead, 6–3. That's when something weird happened.

I took off my cap to scratch my sweaty head. "Ben, what the heck is wrong with your hair?" asked Garrett. "Did your sister experiment on you? Or is this a new look you're trying out?"

"What are you talking about?" I asked, annoyed.

Abhi goggled at me, and his eyes seemed to bulge. "Ben," he whispered. "Your hair!"

"Don't tell me you're in on this," I whispered back.

"It's pink," said Abhi.

"What?" I tried to see, but it was short so I couldn't without a mirror. Then I glanced at a piece of Abhi's hair sticking out from under his cap.

"So's yours!" I exclaimed.

"What?" Abhi took off his cap and tried unsuccessfully to look at his own hair, raising his eyebrows so high I thought they might float off his head. Then he looked over at Garrett. "Garrett, dude, your hair's pink, too!"

It turned out that everyone's hair was pink. Even Trish's. It was bizarre, and we had no explanation. I squinted at Dad standing in the field as first base coach. Was there a pink tinge to his stubble? I rubbed my eyes. I had to be seeing things.

But by the time we were finished batting that inning, everyone's hair color was back to normal. We all decided it must have been a trick of the light. That made more sense than a mass hallucination.

And we won our game, 8–5.

For the next two games, I stepped into my role as the

leader of the Comity Salt Shakers. I almost single-handedly got enough hits and RBI to make our team an unstoppable force. My lucky coin came up heads forty-five times and tails only six. I ignored Trish completely, and she shrunk into the background, barely better than the sixth graders. Abhi hung out with me way more than he did with Trish. Everything was exactly the way I wanted it.

Then why did I feel so miserable?

"What do you think, Ben?" Dad said the morning of our last regular season game. "Should we sign up for the fall?" The town was starting a fall league with just a few teams so kids moving from the small field to the big one could practice before the pressure of the spring league.

"What do you mean, *we*?"

Dad blinked. "If you sign up to play, I'll sign up to coach. I've loved being assistant coach this summer."

"I don't know, Dad. Don't you think you're too busy to be a head coach?"

"Too busy?"

"Yeah. Think of how many times Coach Tom has had to get there early, and he always has to stay late gathering the equipment. You couldn't make a couple of practices, but he has to be there for every single one." My stomach started to roll. Dad was fine as an assistant, but he shouldn't be the one ultimately in charge. I couldn't deal with his constant stream of tips and advice on how to train, how to stand, even how to breathe. And I knew firsthand that he made bad choices.

"I could commit to every practice. It wouldn't be a problem," Dad said. He rubbed the lower part of his chest like something was annoying him.

"Are you okay?" I hadn't seen him do that before. It reminded me eerily of Grandma Beth. My stomach stopped rolling and squeezed down to the size of a ping-pong ball.

Dad stopped. "It's just some indigestion. Probably shouldn't have had that fifth piece of bacon at breakfast," he said.

"Are you sure? Maybe you should get that checked out."

"I'm fine, Ben. Nothing a couple of antacids won't fix."

"But—"

"Time to leave for the game!" Mom said cheerfully as she walked into the room. She had a cooler full of drinks and Fib smiling at the end of his leash.

"Come on, son," Dad said. "Let's go win another game."

Chapter Seventeen

Trish

Stumped and Slumped

Over the next two weeks, I couldn't solve the puzzle. What did demented Tetris blocks have to do with math? I redrew the shapes and tried putting them in different configurations, but the solution didn't become any clearer. Eventually I just tried guessing. The answers so far (one and five) had both been prime, and I knew Ben liked prime numbers. So I tried two, then three, then seven, then eleven. None of them worked. Nothing turned green, and no new puzzle appeared. I was truly stumped.

To make things even worse, I entered the biggest baseball slump of my life. My fastballs were slow and my changeups weren't fooling anyone, no matter how I tried. And I couldn't get a hit to save my life.

The team was happy to eat the snacks I brought from the

Salt Shaker, but now that I wasn't playing well, no one had much to say to me. Ben acted like I didn't exist. Even Abhi kept his distance—probably because he didn't want to upset Ben.

But some really weird stuff was happening. The pink hair incident was strange enough. But in the next game, our whole team sneezed for three minutes in a row. That doesn't sound like a long time, but it truly is when you're sneezing and can barely catch your breath. The opposing team (the Bridgeton Bowl-O-Rama Llamas) laughed their heads off at us wiping our noses and blinking through watery eyes. The ump had to stop the game while we all ran to the community rec building and washed our faces. It must have been some kind of reaction to weird pollen, we thought.

Ben had catapulted himself into becoming the star of the team and led us to two more victories on the field after the pink hair game. I couldn't help admiring how well he was doing. I still wanted to be friends, even if he didn't. Why had I ruined our friendship right when it was starting? Why wouldn't he let me apologize?

In the last game before the playoffs started, we had to face the Bridgeton Camemberts again, this time at home. I handed out the Salt Shaker snacks. Everyone spun their friendship bracelets three times—everyone except Ben, who wasn't wearing his anymore, I noticed with a pang.

Ben ran onto the field, adjusting his cap. His face was open and eager, and it pulled at my heart. Maybe if we managed to win this game, we could find a way to be friends again. For the brief time when we'd gotten along, I'd felt about as happy as I could in Comity.

Baseball feels different every time you play. Some days you have it, and some days you don't. I hoped that I could pull myself out of my slump for our final game of the regular season against our toughest opponents.

We were the home team, so the Camemberts batted first. I was the starting pitcher. The ball felt good in my hand, and I felt well rested and strong. David called for a fastball, and I nodded. I gripped the ball, wound up, and let go.

The batter whacked it for a stand-up double.

I swallowed. It was okay. We were at the very beginning of our game.

But my next pitch, a two-seam fastball, felt sluggish as soon as I let go. And it hit the batter in the thigh. It was the kid Ben called Brick Wall (although I thought his name was Kenny), and he flashed me a grin as he trotted to first base. The umpire called a time-out, came up to me on the mound, and warned me that if I hit another batter, I'd be ejected from the game. I nodded nervously.

But my pitching only got worse from there. I gripped the ball the same and wound up the same as always, but my pitches didn't work the way they used to. I had terrible velocity and even worse control. In the third inning, I came close to accidentally hitting another batter in the head, but he stepped back at the last second. I was mortified; what if I actually hurt someone?

Bridgeton managed to score six runs by the fourth inning, and I couldn't imagine how we'd catch them. They pitched as tough as they batted, and we hadn't scored a single run. I breathed a sigh of relief when Coach Tom said that Abhi would start the fifth. I normally wanted to pitch for as long as possible, but I clearly didn't have the stuff today.

And that was when Ben really upped his game, leading off the bottom of the fifth with a home run against the gigantic unibrowed Camembert pitcher. He was dazzling to watch. "BEN, BEN, BOMBASTIC BEN!" we chanted, joined by all the Comity fans in the crowd. I could hear Aadya's and Asha's whoops, and it made me smile in the middle of my misery.

Led by Ben's brilliance, the rest of the team rose to the occasion. We won the game 7–6 on an RBI double by Abhi in the bottom of the sixth.

No thanks to me, of course. I had let six runs score, and I hadn't gotten a single hit. I plastered on a smile while the rest of the team cheered our amazing accomplishment.

Coach Tom spoke to us briefly about how proud he was, that we'd played like a true team, and he couldn't wait to see what we did next.

"Everyone contributed," said Ben's dad.

Not me, I thought.

"Six wins in a row! We're in great shape heading to the playoffs," said Dad.

Not me.

We'd won, but I had let everyone down.

As we lined up to slap hands with the Camemberts, my mind drifted to the math puzzle again. I still had no idea what it meant. Was it really a math puzzle? And was Ben really the one who had given it to me? I should just ask him. But I couldn't. The last time I'd tried to talk to him, he'd acted like I didn't exist, and I couldn't summon the courage again.

". . . seriously off her game," someone said behind me. My ears pricked.

"What happened? She started the summer off well." It was Andy, one of the sixth graders on our team.

"She's losing it. Lucky she didn't drag us down. She let them score *six runs*. Almost makes me wish she had hit another batter and got kicked off the mound sooner," came Garrett's voice.

My head spun. They were talking trash about me! My own teammates.

I stopped murmuring "good game." I stopped slapping the hands of the Camembert players in line.

I had to get away.

I stepped out of the line, sprinted across the field, and ran into the woods. I plunged into the shade of overhanging trees and the smell of damp earth. Leaves whispered to each other in a language all their own. Hoping to stay hidden, I veered off the path.

Pretty soon, I was lost.

Which made sense, because it was how I'd felt for weeks.

Chapter Eighteen

Ben

Nowhere Girl

"See you in the playoffs," grunted Camembert Unibrow Pitcher #1 as we slapped hands. "Good thing we got your ace's number."

"What's that supposed to mean?" I shot back as I moved to the next guy in line.

"We rattled her today," said Camembert Unibrow Pitcher #2. "Got her throwing at us instead of over the plate."

"She hit *one* guy," I grumbled. "That can happen to anyone." I hadn't meant to defend Trish, but it was true.

"We'll light her up again next time," said Raccoon Face. "If you don't lose and get kicked out of the playoffs before you even face us."

"Not a chance. We're going to face off again, and she'll shut you guys down. It'll be a miracle if you even score two runs off her in the playoffs," I said. I wasn't Trish's biggest fan at the moment, but I knew more than anyone that one bad game, or even four bad games, didn't make you a bad player.

"How'd you get so good all of a sudden?" asked the Incredible Hulk of a Catcher.

"I don't know. How'd you get so ugly?" I flinched and waited for him to punch me in the nose. But to my shock, he just glared at me and moved on.

The rest of them, at least, had the sense not to say anything other than "good game."

The team went back to the dugout to pack up.

"We should go get lunch and celebrate," said Abhi. He glanced around. "Where's Trish?"

I also looked around but didn't see her. Trish's dad was still on the field talking to Coach Tom and Dad.

"Have you seen Trish?" Abhi asked George, who shrugged his shoulders.

Well, she couldn't be far. Her dad was still here.

Fib ran to me just as I started zipping up my bag. He wiggled in a full-body wag, and his tongue almost touched the ground in a big doggy smile. He sat next to my bag and put a heavy paw on my leg.

"Hey there, good boy," I said as I shook his paw.

Fib put his paw down, then picked it up and put both feet on my thighs.

"I don't have any treats, sorry. Down," I said as I pushed

him off. "Want to eat lunch at my house?" I turned my head to ask Abhi.

The next moment, I felt something ram into my legs, and I flipped over the bench and crashed onto my back. Fib jumped on top of me and lay on my chest, his breath in my face and an intense look in his eyes. His pupils were so big I could have fallen into them.

"Fib, what is wrong with you?" I spluttered as Abhi cracked up.

"Looks like he really wants something. You sure you don't have any treats?" Abhi said.

"Fib, get off." I tried to shove him, but he seemed unusually dense.

His face got closer to me, and his teeth gleamed. There was no way my sweet old dog, the one who'd known me since I was a baby, was going to bite me.

Right?

"Fib!" I struggled, but he wouldn't budge.

Fib's mouth opened, and he licked my entire face. Then he leaped off me, stuck his head in my sports bag, and took off with something in his mouth.

"Fib!"

I scrambled to my feet. "Stop him!" I cried.

Abhi tried to grab Fib, but he dodged him and raced out of the dugout, out into the open field, and into the woods.

I dug through my bag. He had taken the math puzzle book! I'd put it in there so I could try to sneak peeks at the next problem in case the game got slow.

"I've got to go get him!" I said as I started out of the dugout.

"He'll come back eventually, right? He doesn't usually wander too far," said Abhi.

I shook my head. "He's been acting weird lately, spending hours roaming in the woods."

"Want some help?" Abhi asked.

"It shouldn't take me long to find him. Tell my dad, okay? We can hang out once I'm back."

"Sure, dude. No problem."

I ran into the woods.

I followed the path from Bailey Park back toward home, whistling and calling Fib's name. The woods seemed strangely quiet, like even the birds and animals were watching and waiting for something. Fib could be anywhere, I realized. He could evade me for hours in here. Since his arthritis had been magically cured, I wasn't worried about his safety. But I was worried about that math book. I needed it for the playoffs. My team needed it. I knew it was responsible for my sudden prowess on the baseball field, and we couldn't win without it.

After running for several minutes, I heard a whine to my

left, and I veered off the path in the direction I thought it came from. I passed through a thick tangle of trees and vines, until I came out of the foliage to a big pond I'd never seen in Comity Woods. On the other side of the pond was an enormous tree. I heard another whine and moved closer. I had never seen anything like the tree before; in addition to having a gigantic trunk, its branches spread out in all directions, and some of them shot down to the ground to form trunks themselves. It was like an entire family of trees, clustered together and living under the same canopy of leaves.

"Fib?" I called. "You there, boy? Come out. It's okay, I'm not mad."

The whining had stopped, but I heard a different noise as I got closer to the tree. And as I made my way around the enormous trunk, I realized what it was.

Trish was leaning with her forehead against the tree and sobbing like her heart was breaking. Fib stood at her feet, pressing his body against her legs and whining softly from time to time.

My mouth went dry, and I froze in my tracks. I didn't want to see Trish like this. I took a step back, hoping I could sneak off before she noticed me. But the crack of a branch gave me away.

Trish whipped her head up. "What do you want? Am I kicked off the team?" Her voice was thick.

"What are you talking about?" I wiped my sweaty palms on my pants.

She took a shuddering breath, wiped her face, and looked at me with red eyes. I rubbed the spot on my wrist where her bracelet used to be.

"Did you guys have fun, then? Talking about me behind my back?"

"Who's talking—"

"I heard them, Ben. They didn't even try to hide it! They were making fun of me, saying I'd lost my touch and nearly lost the game."

"Don't pay attention to those Bridgeton guys—"

"It wasn't Bridgeton guys! It was people on our team!" She clenched her fists.

"Okay, okay." I held my hands up. "Who?"

"Andy and Connor," she sniffed. "And . . . and Garrett."

"Trish. You're talking about *Garrett*. He's a jerk no matter what happens. He said the same stuff about me when I wasn't playing so great."

"This is what I knew would happen."

"What do you mean? You're the best player on our team."

Trish straightened up, looked me in the eye, and crossed her arms. Her hair was just getting long enough to curl at her neck.

"Not lately. You don't understand what it's like to always

be the odd one out. The only girl on a baseball team. Or on a math team. Always. People wait for you to screw up."

"I—"

"I have to be perfect," she said, her voice breaking. "I can't win, Ben. We've moved four times in six years. Each time I start someplace new, I need to be the best at everything—math and baseball—to even be on a team. But if I stay the best, people resent me. And if I slip up, even a little bit, they want to kick me out. My previous Math Puzzler team was full of eighth grade boys who were mad when I made the team and their friend didn't. But I proved myself to them, and they respected me. Same with my baseball team. When I moved this time, I knew I'd have to start all over again, and I was so scared I couldn't do it. That's why I chopped off all my hair. I wanted to be a different person, one who could find a place where I felt at home."

"Trish—"

"There's no place in the world where I belong. Not South Ridgefield. Not Comity. Not on the Math Puzzler team. And apparently not on the baseball field, either." She covered her face with her hands.

"I'm glad you're on our team," I said quietly. Weirdly, I realized it was true.

"You don't act like it. Ever," she said from behind her hands.

She was right. But I didn't want to admit it. Instead I said,

"Think of all the good stuff that's happened this summer. We're in a great position for the playoffs. We beat the Camemberts today."

"No thanks to me."

"That's why we're a team. No one's perfect all the time. When one of us is off our game, other people have to step up. Your pitching kept us in the game. And . . . and think about the Math Puzzler Championship," I said. "You got the Individual Prize." It surprised me that it didn't hurt to think about it anymore.

Trish looked at me with such pain in her eyes that I winced.

"I have to tell you something," she said. "You already hate me, so—"

"I don't hate you. I mean, not really . . ."

"Ben, just let me finish, okay? Then you can tell me whether you hate me or not."

I nodded.

Trish took a shuddering breath and started talking fast. "You remember how I beat you by just one point? Well, when the Math Puzzler tournament people sent us the answer sheet, I looked it over. And I realized something," she said. "Remember that third problem?"

"Ugh, it was so tough. It was one of the two I got wrong," I said.

The rest of Trish's words tumbled out in a rush. "They

had marked my answer to that problem right when it wasn't. I didn't actually win the Individual Prize, Ben. But I didn't contact them to correct their mistake. And then we moved. And the longer I went without telling them, the harder it was to do. I *hate* cheating. I hate it more than anything! But it turns out I'm the biggest cheater there is. I've been so embarrassed. I haven't told anyone—not my parents, not even Sanjay. I decided not to try out for the Math Puzzler team this year, as punishment. But then I met you, and it's been so much fun thinking about math puzzles with you. That is, before I messed everything up." She gave a half laugh that turned into a sob. "So now you know everything you should hate me for." Tears streamed down her face again, and she didn't even try to wipe them away.

What?

After all the agony I'd been through thinking I had failed at the Math Puzzler tournament, after losing that bet with Abhi and signing up for summer ball, now I find out that Trish *didn't even win*?

"So what you're saying is . . . we tied?" I asked.

Trish wiped her face on her sleeve and nodded. She seemed absolutely miserable.

Say what's in your heart, the book said. Well, I was going to. I took a deep breath.

"I'm glad we tied."

Trish's eyes were large and dark. "What?"

"I said, I'm glad we tied. Because you're the best math puzzler I know, and if I tied you, that's pretty awesome. And if I hadn't thought you won the Individual Prize, I wouldn't be playing baseball at all this summer. Probably not ever."

"What do you mean?" Trish scrunched her eyebrows again.

"Abhi had been on me about signing up for baseball, but I didn't want to after . . . after the last season I played. So I made a bet with him. I promised that if I lost the Math Puzzler Individual Prize, I would sign up for summer ball. I hated being on our team at first, but now I remember why I love baseball so much. I love all the numbers, of course, the stats and the scoring. But baseball had lost its magic, and you helped bring it back for me."

Trish nodded. "Baseball's always been a bit magical to me, too, and I don't even believe in magic."

"I'm sorry I've been such a jerk. You love math puzzles and baseball as much as I do. It was hard to see what we had in common instead of feeling like I was competing with you all over again. I should have been friendlier to you from the very beginning. If only . . ."

"I weren't such a perfectionist pain?" Trish asked.

I raised my eyebrows. "Yeah, maybe. Also, I could try not being so stubborn."

Suddenly, Fib pointed his nose in the air and barked.

Trish burst out laughing, and it was kind of contagious. I snickered, then laughed, and finally threw my head back and howled until my knees got weak.

When we finally stopped, Trish was sprawled on the ground with her back against the giant tree, and Fib had climbed into her lap.

"He's so sweet," said Trish, stroking Fib's reddish-brown fur. "He found me and made me feel better right away. Like I wasn't so alone in the world." Fib nestled his head into the crook of her elbow.

I swallowed. "You're not. Alone, I mean."

Trish looked at me, and this time all I saw was gratitude.

"If anyone should have been kicked off our team, it was me," I said.

"You're one of our best players!"

"But I was lousy in the beginning. You've been a great teammate since day one. You never said anything bad to me, even when I couldn't catch an easy pop-up or get my bat on the ball. We wouldn't have a shot at winning the tournament without you. No one wants to kick you off the team. And if they did, I wouldn't let them."

Trish stayed silent for a long time and kept her head down. I worried she'd start bawling again.

"You don't think I don't belong on the field? Because I'm a girl?"

I shook my head and laughed. “I’m the last guy to say a girl can’t play baseball. Especially someone who loves it as much as you do.”

And that was the truth.

“What’s that supposed to mean, you’re the last guy?”

I looked away. I didn’t want to talk about it.

“Does it have anything to do with why you stopped playing ball two years ago?”

Chapter Nineteen

Trish

The Last Game

Ben ran his hand up the back of his head so his hair stood on end, then jammed his cap back on. "You really want to know?"

I nodded.

"Come on," he said. "Let's start heading back so our parents don't freak out. I'll tell you on the way."

Fib led us to the path that led back to Bailey.

"You know who taught me how to play baseball?" Ben asked.

"Your dad?" Although I wondered about that, since I noticed Ben hardly spoke to his dad at games.

Ben shook his head. "It was my dad's mom, Grandma Beth."

My surprise must have shown on my face.

"Grandma Beth wasn't like other grandmothers," Ben said.

"Sure, she hosted us for holidays and took Claudia shopping for clothes and other horrible stuff. But she *got* me. And she loved baseball. Watching it and playing it."

"Sounds like she was pretty awesome."

"Yeah." Ben smiled, and his face brightened. "Grandma Beth's mom, Shirley, had played in the All-American Girls Professional Baseball League in the 1940s."

"No way! I'm reading a book on that right now! Those women were incredible. So your grandma played baseball, too? Like her mom?"

Ben nodded. "In the 1960s, Grandma Beth played Little League baseball in her town even though there were no other girls on her team. At first, she said, she tucked her hair into her cap and said her name was Bobby. Once she knew she'd made the team, she told her coach, who was surprised but said as long as she could keep up, she could play."

"That's so cool," I said.

Ben smiled. "She was the only girl baseball player in the state, I think. She always told me she had to work harder and smarter. That since she knew she'd never be the strongest, she had to use every other tool she had."

I nodded. "That's what Sanjay always tells me."

"She played right up until she was eleven, when a tournament umpire told her coach that if he didn't get rid of her, their team would forfeit. And that was the end of her baseball career."

I stopped walking. "That's so unfair!" I was going to have to give up baseball soon, I knew. But at least it was on my own terms and not because someone told me I wasn't allowed to play.

"I know," said Ben. We started moving again. "But Grandma Beth never gave up on loving baseball. She taught all her kids to play, and any grandkids who were interested. Every Thanksgiving my older cousins and I play a big game together while we wait for the turkey to be done. Claudia's not into any kind of sports, but I love baseball. I've loved it forever."

"Me, too," I said. "It's the best game there is."

"And Grandma Beth explained baseball in ways I could understand. And she helped me use math to calm myself down when I was tempted to psych myself out."

"Like counting primes as a way to focus?"

"Yeah." Ben gave me a half smile. "And calculating my batting average and my ERA when I pitched. She was the best coach I ever had. Dad was so serious about everything, and that always made me nervous. And he wouldn't stop giving me baseball advice, like 24/7. He always wanted me to do things *his* way. But Grandma Beth helped me find the ways that worked for *me*. When I was little and afraid of getting hit by a ball, she threw one way up in the air and let it hit her smack in the chest. I was terrified! But she just laughed and told me it hurt but not that much."

Fib led us around a huge tree.

"Anyway, two years ago my team played the town AAA spring championship on the day after I finished fourth grade. It was the perfect evening, sunny but not too hot, with just a few cotton candy clouds in a bright blue sky. Know what I mean?"

"Yeah," I breathed. Perfect baseball weather.

"Dad was head coach, and Grandma was one of his assistants. Dad told me I was going to be the starting pitcher."

"I thought you didn't pitch?" I asked.

"I did then." Ben raised his eyebrows. "I was nowhere near the best pitcher on the team. Even back then, Abhi was clearly our best bet. But Dad said I'd be fine, and that we needed to lead with our lefty ace." Ben turned to me and fixed me to the ground with his bright blue stare. "When I think about it now, I know the problem was that Dad always thought I was better than I really was."

I blinked. "Oh, I'm sure he—"

"It's like a movie that plays over and over in my head. I let nine runs score in the first three innings."

Yikes! "A bad game happens to everyone—"

"And then with Abhi pitching the fourth, I made an error at first base that let another run score." Ben sounded like he didn't want to get to the end of the story but needed to tell it just the same. "But we were able to battle back and get the game close again, until I came up to bat at the bottom of the sixth with the score 10–9 and two outs. I just needed a single—or a walk, anything but an out—to keep us alive. The top of the order, our best hitters, were coming up."

I held my breath.

Ben clenched his jaw. "I struck out swinging. It was over."

"Man, that stinks."

Ben nodded. "Dad and the other coaches talked to us about how we'd tried our hardest and should be proud. But they didn't tell the truth."

"What does that mean?"

"We lost because of me."

I shook my head. "Ben, one person's not—"

"Me, and Dad."

I let the words sink in. "Okay, so maybe your dad didn't make the world's best coaching decisions. But it was because he loves you and believes in you."

Ben waved at me to stop. "Let me finish." His eyes were faraway. "Grandma Beth said the same thing you did. 'That's the way it goes sometimes,' she said. But when she put her hand on my cheek, it trembled. Dad said we were still going out for pizza. But Grandma said her stomach was bothering her, and she was going to turn in early. She pulled me aside and said she was proud of me. She said she knew how I felt. 'Remember, Ben, that baseball is designed to break your heart.

But we love it anyway, because it fills our hearts, too.' She said that once I was done feeling down, I needed to get out there again."

"She was right," I said. "So why did you quit?"

"Because that was the last time I saw Grandma Beth."

Chapter Twenty

Ben

The Golden Ratio

"What happened?"

I swallowed. I hadn't talked about it in two years. Actually, I wasn't sure I'd talked about it to anyone outside my family. Other than Abhi, of course. "She went to bed and never woke up. Turns out that funny feeling in her stomach was a heart attack. Dad and I should've realized something was wrong. But instead of checking on her, Dad spent the whole night talking about our plans for summer ball, and how we'd work on pitching even more."

Trish's eyes sparkled with tears. "Oh, Ben. I'm so, so sorry. I bet she'd be proud of you now. You're playing baseball again. And you're amazing!"

I smiled half-heartedly. I wasn't sure what Grandma Beth would think about the magical math book making me that way. I let out a big breath. “She’d be thrilled about a girl player who’s as incredible as you are. Sorry I’ve been so awful to you.”

Trish grinned. “I don’t think I made it easy for you. That This Is a Stick riddle . . . I thought it would be something you’d like.”

“Forget about it,” I said. I couldn’t believe I’d gotten that mad about a dumb game. “You know how you said you were tired of having to start over in a new place all the time? Well, at the beginning of the summer, I’d have given anything to start over in a place where no one knew me. A place where people didn’t know that I choked when it was important. Garrett hasn’t been able to stand me since that championship game, but I feel like the whole town will never forget what happened.”

“It was just one game, Ben. Any team can lose, and any player can have a bad day,” Trish said.

“Since that game, every time I thought of playing baseball, it reminded me of how terrible I was in that game, and how Dad refused to take me out as pitcher. We lost, and then we lost Grandma. I just . . . I didn’t ever want to play again. But here I am, and now we have a chance to win the tournament. If we’re lucky enough to get that far, we’ll face probably the Camemberts in the final round. They’ve been so awful to both of us. We need to *win*. And then maybe I can really put that awful game from two years ago behind me forever."

Trish tilted her head. "Ben, even if we play well, we may not win the tournament."

I nodded. "I still want to try. I just don't want to choke. So I'm asking for your help. We've got to get this team into the best shape possible, and play our hearts out in the tournament."

Trish stood tall and straight. "Count me in." Then she smiled. "I really want to beat the Camemberts, too."

Fib trotted up to Trish with the math book in his mouth. I tried to grab it, but Trish got there first. She glanced at the book and cried, "I knew it!"

All the blood drained out of my head. Trish knew about the magical math book?

She tilted her head and squinted at me. "You made one for yourself, too? Or is this one you gave someone else on the team?"

"What are you talking about?"

Trish showed me the book. "*The Mathematics of The Wild*. Did you put a copy of this in my mailbox or did someone give it to you, too? How did you get the invisible ink to work?"

I put my hands up. "I didn't give it to you. And I certainly didn't write it! I didn't even know that you got one, too!" Trish hadn't gotten any miraculous baseball powers from her book. Maybe because she was already so good?

Trish blinked. "But then who . . ."

"I'm not sure. But I know one thing: that book is magic."

Trish giggled. "Very funny. It's got some great riddles. I'm stuck on one, though. Haven't been able to figure it out for a couple weeks."

I caught my breath. "Trish! Maybe that's why you've been struggling with your baseball playing lately!"

Trish narrowed her eyes. "You think my pitching got bad because I couldn't figure out a *math puzzle*?"

I nodded. "I'm not kidding. I don't know who sent us these books, but ever since I started solving those math problems, I've been amazing at baseball. Does the ink turn green when you solve a puzzle, and does it show you a sentence?"

Trish blinked. "Yeah, but—"

"My first sentence was, *Say it out loud.* So I did, and that was how I finally figured out that puzzle you'd given me with the ones and twos."

"But—"

I kept going. She needed to hear the whole thing before she told me I was crazy. "And then I . . . kind of *spoke* to the ball in the next game. When the pitch came in, I told it to move right over the plate. And it *did*. That's when I hit that monster home run. And I've been unstoppable ever since. Even my lucky coin knows! See? It's definitely magic."

We arrived back at Bailey. "Ben," said Trish. "There's no such thing as magic. I'm sure you've gotten better at hitting because of all the practice you've been putting in. As for the books, maybe the Math Puzzler people sent these to us? But whoever did, I need help with mine. Want to work on the problems together?"

She was wrong, I knew it. The books were magical for sure, and we needed them to win.

But I played it cool and shrugged. "Sure."

Trish and Abhi both came to lunch at my house after the game.

"So things are good between you two now? Finally?" Abhi asked.

"Yeah," Trish said. "We talked in the woods while we brought Fib back."

"Now we can concentrate on getting ready for the playoffs," I said. "We need to call extra practices."

"Great idea," Dad said as he came into the kitchen. "I can take off early from work, and run pitching and batting drills. Your fielding is already excellent—"

"Dad," I said. "We are calling the extra practices. Just the kids. We don't need you."

Dad took a step back and looked like I'd hit him in the head with a fastball. "Oh," he said.

Trish glanced between us. "Thanks anyway, Mr. Messina. We'll still have our two practices with you, my dad, and Coach

Tom, but we wanted to hold some kids-only practices so we could bond better as a team."

Dad nodded. "I understand. Okay, we'll try my drills during the regular practices, then." He left the room looking slightly bewildered.

"Dude, that was harsh. He's our coach, and your dad. We do need him," Abhi said.

"I don't," I said.

That night, Abhi, Trish, and I contacted the rest of the players on a group text, and everyone on our team but one of the sixth graders (whose name I still couldn't remember) agreed to come to our extra practices. Even Garrett. The next day, Abhi and Trish came over to strategize over Salt Shaker snacks.

"We'll probably have to get through two rounds to make it to the championship game, since our record is 6–4. The Camemberts will get top seed for sure, since they only lost two games," Abhi said.

"One of which was to us," I said with a grin. "But you're right. With six teams, the first round will knock out three of us. Then the top team left will get a bye while the other two teams play each other to see who gets to face them."

"The Camemberts have seen me pitch twice now," said Trish. "And they hit me hard yesterday. If we face them in the championship game, I don't know if I should pitch."

"But you're our best pitcher!" Abhi said in a horrified voice.

"Let's just worry about that when we get to it," I said, surprising myself with how calm I was. "What do we want to do during these practices?" I dipped a truffle fry in garlic aioli (fancy garlic mayo, basically) and got ready to write down our ideas.

Fib came over and shamelessly laid his head in Trish's lap.

"Get out of here, you mooch," I said.

"I don't mind," said Trish, stroking his head. "He's comforting. And he brings people together, this dog." She gazed at Fib. "I love this mark on his head."

"A Fibonacci spiral, right?" said Abhi. "Just one of the weird math things I know because of Ben."

"What weird math things?" asked Mom, coming into the kitchen. "Anything I should know about?"

"We're just talking about the spiral on Fib's head," I said.

Fib tore himself away from Trish and trotted to Mom, who made a big deal out of him and scratched him under the chin.

"How does the spiral link to Fibonacci numbers?" asked Abhi. "I'm sure you told me this before, but I forget."

"Here," said Mom. She took a piece of paper and started drawing. "We know that the first few numbers in the Fibonacci sequence are 0, 1, 1, 2, 3, 5, 8, 13, 21, and so on, right? We can create a pattern of squares where the sides are Fibonacci numbers, and arrange them. If you draw lines connecting the diagonals of these squares, they form a spiral, like this."

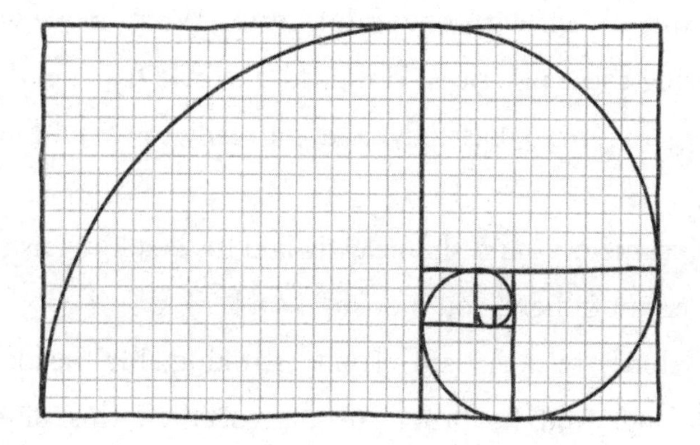

"Right! That's exactly what the spiral on Fib's head looks like," said Trish, reaching over to stroke Fib while his tail swept the floor like a furry windshield wiper.

"And these spirals occur over and over in nature, from seedheads to pine cone sections to hurricanes," I said.

"Same with the Fibonacci numbers themselves," said Trish. "I wonder why."

"Ah," said Mom, smiling. "That has to do with the golden ratio, or Phi. If you divide each Fibonacci number by the one before it, you approach, but never reach, an irrational number that goes on forever," said Mom.

"Which is approximately 1.61803," I said.

"But what does that have to do with flower petals and leaves?" asked Abhi.

"It means that it's not the numbers themselves that are the most important thing," said Mom. "It's the ratio between them."

Trish jumped up like she just figured out the secret to the universe. "Could it be that the spiral, the number of petals or leaves—they're all arranged that way to maximize each petal or leaf's exposure to the sun, bees, and whatever else the plants need? It's about what's best for the whole plant, rather than each leaf."

"Exactly," said Mom. "Let me know if you'd like to substitute-lecture for me sometime."

Trish giggled. "Thanks, Dr. Messina."

"I'll let you guys get back to work." Mom winked at us, then grabbed a granola bar and left the kitchen.

"Back to planning for our practice tonight," I said. "How do we want to run things?"

"That's easy," said Abhi. "Let's maximize everyone's exposure to the sun."

Trish and I stared at him, confused.

"Let's get everyone doing what they're best at, so everyone contributes to the team," said Abhi.

That was it. We wrote down our plan.

That evening, Abhi, Trish, and I led the first practice without our coaches. Garrett gave me a look as he smacked his glove with his fist.

"There are a few things we should get straight before we start," I said. I was nervous; everyone had shown up, but would they pay attention? Would they pay attention to *me*? I took a deep breath and continued. "We're a team, and we need to act like one. We root for each other, and we don't gossip behind each other's backs." I glared at Garrett and the sixth grade contingent, and I was gratified to see Garrett's neck turn pink above his collar. He opened his mouth, but I kept talking.

"Second, whatever stuff we've said about each other stays in the past. We're moving forward, okay? Clean slate."

The team murmured yes. Garrett closed his mouth and gave me a nod.

"Because we really have a shot at winning, and I really want to show Bridgeton what a Comity team can do."

"And maybe if we're good enough, we'll all get to meet the Turkeys," said George.

Everyone cheered.

"Okay. Let's split up. I'm going to work on batting, Abhi will do running and fielding drills over there, and Trish will be working with the pitchers."

"How come Trish is running the pitching drills?" asked Garrett. Great, he was going to be a pain.

"Because she's the best pitcher on our team," Abhi shot back coolly.

No one had any other questions.

I smiled as I headed to the mound to throw for batting practice. No matter what happened in the playoffs, I wasn't a loser anymore.

Chapter Twenty-One

Trish

Playoffs and Puzzles

I didn't believe in magical books. There was no way solving math puzzles made Ben better at baseball. It had to be because of all his hard work. Right?

It didn't matter that we didn't know who sent us the math books, or that Ben believed they were mystical. What mattered was that the math puzzles cemented our friendship, and we had finally told each other the truth. Now maybe I could work up the courage to tell Mom.

But Mom was working harder than ever, and was barely home for me to tell her anything. She was off to work before I woke up in the morning, and often came home after I'd gone to sleep. One night, I woke to voices in the hallway outside my room.

"She wants you to come to a game this weekend," Dad said.

"You've only been to one all summer."

"I need to cover the cath lab again," said Mom.

"Amrita, you need to take a break, for your own sake."

"I need to make sure things are running smoothly. It'll be better soon. I've had some tough cases lately. There are some things that can't be healed, and in my lab, I want to find a way to heal them."

"Trish needs you now," said Dad. "She's only going to be twelve once. And baseball is really important to her."

"I can't wait until she's done with baseball. She's spending so much time on it."

"Because she loves it. And she loves you, and wants you to be proud of her."

"I am proud of her. I just . . . I want her to focus on what's really important."

"She is," said Dad. "She's a leader on the team. You should come watch her play."

"We'll see," Mom said.

I kept my eyes closed as they opened the door. Dad kissed my forehead and left, but Mom lingered by the side of the bed.

I wanted to open my eyes and tell her about what had happened at the Math Puzzler tournament, about what it was like being the only girl again on a baseball team, about how I'd finally made friends in Comity. But I didn't. I couldn't. If she wanted me to talk to her, maybe she should try being in a room with me while I was awake. And what if my confessing my secret disappointed her? What if she thought I was another broken thing she couldn't heal?

Finally, Mom leaned over and kissed my cheek. "I love you, Trisha," she said.

When I woke in the morning, she was already gone.

In terms of friends, the week leading up to the playoffs was the best of the summer. Ben, Abhi, and I worked together on math puzzles and baseball. Abhi wasn't the most experienced math puzzler, but he was smart and had fun trying to figure out the problems with us.

Ben and Abhi were just as baffled by the puzzle that had stumped me, but we solved a couple more from Ben's book. First there was this one:

182^ = 13

90^ = 9

30^ = 5

6^ = ?

I solved it this way:

182^ = 13, so ^ = 13/182 = 1/14

90^ = 9, so ^ = 9/90 = 1/10

30^ = 5, so ^ = 5/30 = 1/6

For 13, ^ was 1/14

For 9, ^ was 1/10

For 5, ^ was 1/6

So for 6, were there two numbers next to each other whose product equaled six? Yes! 2 and 3. So 6^ = 2

And then, checking, if 6^ = 2

^ = 2/6 = 1/3

But Ben had solved it a different way. He'd noticed that:

$$13 \times 13 + 13 = 182$$

$$9 \times 9 + 9 = 90$$

$$5 \times 5 + 5 = 30$$

So, what × what + what = 6?

2 × 2 + 2!

We wrote *2*, and the puzzle turned green. And then came a sentence:

Work together.

Abhi bought Ben's magic theory completely, but I just couldn't believe it. There had to be some sort of sophisticated ink, or maybe a microprocessor, in the pages. There had to be a logical explanation.

In any case, we were having a great time working together.

Like the math puzzles, baseball was clicking for our team. Our two regular practices with the coaches were fine, but we bonded better as a team when we practiced on our own. We had our speediest players (George and Abhi, but also Campbell, who was surprisingly quick) practice strategies for stealing bases. We worked on bunting (always an essential skill, and one a defense would have a hard time guarding against), and we worked hard on making sure all our pitchers were throwing as confidently as possible.

I went to the Salt Shaker every day to pick up snacks for the team. In addition to Luna, who still wouldn't accept any money, the entire Salt Shaker crew seemed to be involved in making them. But kids kept having weird reactions during our practices—breaking out in purple blotches that disappeared after a few minutes; hiccuping intermittently for an afternoon; even growing fuzzy hair on our forearms that resembled a donkey's fur. I began to get the sneaking suspicion that these were all somehow a result of the Salt Shaker snacks, but when I mentioned this, all the guys reacted in horror.

"The snacks bring us luck," said George. "We couldn't win a game before we started eating them, and we definitely won't have a chance in the playoffs without them."

"Yeah, and these . . . funny effects don't last very long," Garrett said, petting the gray fur on his forearm fondly.

"Something wrong, Garrett?" asked Coach Tom.

Garrett hurried to throw his sweatshirt over his arm. "Everything's fine, Coach."

There was a lot riding on the first round of the playoffs. This was our chance to see if all our practice had paid off.

I'd had plenty of rest even though I was normally sleepless before a big game. Maybe I was too relaxed? We were facing the Banbury Bakery Buns, and we'd done well against them in our previous game, so I felt confident . . . I hoped I wasn't *too* confident. But my fastball was fast, my two-seamer broke well, and my changeup was well disguised. I managed to pitch a shutout, and we won 1–0 off Ben's solo home run in the fourth.

"I knew we'd win," Ben said. "The lucky coin came up twenty-three heads to two tails."

After the game, Ben, Abhi, and I went to Ben's house and moved on to the next math puzzle in his book:

1 + 🌳 × 🌳 = 17

4 × 🐿️ × 🐿️ = 36

🌳 × 🐿️ × 🌰 + 🌰 + 🌰 = 72

🌳 − 🐿️ + 🌰 = ?

This was tricky, but not as hard as some of the other puzzles we'd seen. First, we solved the first line:

1 + 🌳 × 🌳 = 17

We subtracted 1 from each side to get

🌳 × 🌳 = 16

We knew the square root of 16 is 4, so 🌳 = 4.

Next, the second line:

4 × 🐿 × 🐿 = 36

We divided each side by 4 to get

🐿 × 🐿 = 9

Once again, we knew the square root of 9 is 3, so

🐿 = 3

"*Squirrel squared* has to be one of the funniest things ever," I said in a fit of giggles. Ben and Abhi laughed right along with me.

After we wiped our eyes, we moved on to the third line:

🌳 × 🐿 × 🌰 + 🌰 + 🌰 = 72

We plugged in the numbers for what knew about tree and squirrel:

4 × 3 × 🌰 + 🌰 + 🌰 = 72

12 × 🌰 + 🌰 + 🌰 = 72

We divided both sides by 12 to get

🌰 + 🌰 + 🌰 = 6

So 🌰 = 2

Finally, we plugged everything into the last equation:

🌳 – 🐿 + 🌰 = ?

4 – 3 + 2 = 3

"You know, when it's about puzzles, math is actually kind of fun," Abhi said.

Ben clapped him on the back. "Try out for the Math Puzzler team in the fall, dude."

We wrote the answer in the book (it was another prime number!). Once again, the answer turned green. And another sentence appeared:

Look to the whole.

None of us had any idea what that meant.

And then, finally, Ben's book showed the same problem as mine, the problem that stumped us all:

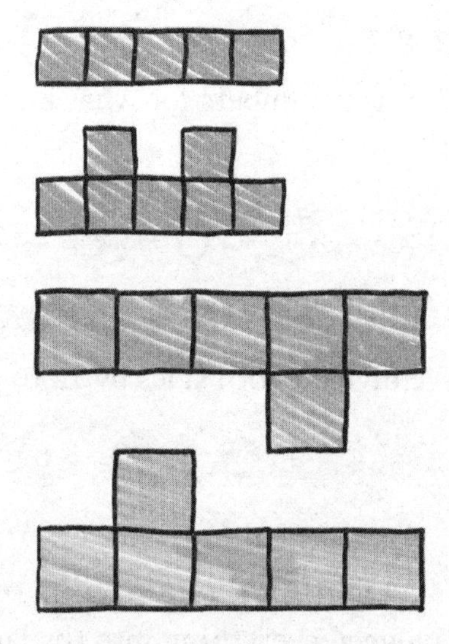

"What do Tetris pieces have to do with math?" Abhi asked.

Ben squinted at the page. "Something seems familiar," he said. "But I can't figure out what it is."

We didn't know how to begin finding the solution. We couldn't even figure out the question.

In the second playoff game, we faced the Bridgeton Bowl-O-Rama Llamas. Abhi's sisters arrived decked out in Salt Shaker green, blue, and white, with ten string bracelets on each of their arms. Rob and Luna were both at the game standing next to a tall, silver-haired man. Ben enthralled our whole team before the game, flipping an astounding forty-nine to two heads to tails on his lucky coin.

Abhi pitched brilliantly deep into the fourth inning until he walked three batters in a row to load the bases. David relieved him and pitched his way out of that jam, and we ended up winning 8–2 as what seemed like the entire town of Comity cheered us on.

We went back to the math puzzle that night. We tried writing random prime numbers as the solution, but none of them were correct. We couldn't begin to understand what the symbols meant. But Ben didn't get frustrated or upset, even when none of our ideas were right. Gone was the Ben who would stop talking to me for the flimsiest reason.

We were finally friends for real. Abhi and me. Ben and me. Ben, Abhi, and me.

"We're Primes," I said.

Abhi grinned, and Ben's smile made his eyes sparkle. "Primes," they said, bumping my fists.

But all of this was just a prelude to what we knew would be the biggest game of the summer. As we'd predicted, we were facing the Bridgeton Cheese Shop Camemberts in the championship game. I didn't believe in magic . . . but I couldn't help hoping for some.

Chapter Twenty-Two

Ben

Lost and Found

Trish asked me to visit the Salt Shaker with her before the big championship game. I was happy to help her out—the guys wanted an extra-large supply of chips and fries to keep us strong while we faced the Bridgeton Camemberts again. And I was curious; I'd never needed to visit the store before since Trish had always kept us well supplied with snacks.

It was good we could use the back entrance because the place was mobbed. I followed Trish into a tiny, immaculate kitchen with a big glass window that opened to the main part of the store. The guys who worked there were like machines, chopping and frying and spicing and bagging efficiently, not a motion wasted or a step out of place. And everything was weirdly hushed, which made me feel like we were in a library.

"What do we do now?" I whispered to Trish.

"We just wait for Luna to bring us our snacks," she whispered back.

"There you are, Trish," came a voice.

A girl with pale green hair and strange yellow cat eyes came into the room trailed by two other Salt Shaker employees, each with different colored hair (pink and purple), carrying at least a dozen paper bags between them.

"Here's your order, plus a few extra bags of Sports Crisps, for good measure. I hope you have an excellent game." Her helpers set the bags down on a small table.

"Thanks so much," said Trish. "Are you coming to watch the game?"

"I will try. But it's so busy right now; it might be hard for me to break away."

"This is my teammate Ben. He's the one I told you about."

"A pleasure, Ben. I'm Luna."

"Nice to meet you," I said. I hoped we could get out quickly; I was itching to leave and get mentally prepared for the game, since I knew the Camemberts would play dirty if they had to. I took a couple of snack bags and unzipped my sports duffel to stow them inside since Trish and I couldn't possibly carry everything with just our hands. Since there was absolutely no parking near the store, Sanjay was meeting us a few streets over to drive us to Bridgeton nice and early. Dad was disappointed that I wasn't riding with him, but it was better this way.

"Ben's your fellow math puzzler, right?" Luna asked.

Trish nodded. "Yes, and the star of our baseball team. He's hit so many home runs, we can't keep track! And we both love math at least as much as we love baseball. Right, Ben?"

I could feel my face heating up. I nodded, shifting my glove aside in my bag to make room. The math book poked out, and I tried to shove it back in. If only we could make headway on that problem. It seemed ridiculous that we couldn't figure it out, even working together. There must be some trick we were missing.

"What's that?" Luna's voice cut through the air sharply. She stared at my bag with those freaky eyes of hers.

"Just my baseball stuff," I said, reaching for more snacks.

"No. I mean, what about that book?" asked Luna.

"I . . . nothing," I said, trying to shove the math book farther down.

"It's a math puzzle book," Trish said cheerfully. "Ben and I have been working on it in our spare time. It's really cool, with invisible ink and everything. We're stumped on a puzzle right now, though."

"Are you, now?" Luna said, narrowing her eyes. "Can I take a look?"

"We need to get going," I said.

"We've got some time," Trish said. "It can't hurt to show Luna. Maybe she can help." She took the math book and held it out.

Luna's eyes widened as she took the book and flipped

through it. "You've made quite a bit of progress, I see," she said. "This is such an unusual book. Where did you find it?"

"They just showed up in our mailboxes," Trish said.

"There are *two* of them?" Luna's voice went higher.

"Yeah, I've got one almost exactly like it. The problems are in a different order, though."

"Very good, boys, keep up the excellent work," came a voice. "If we continue to go along like this, we'll have no problem at all defeating them. *And there the snake throws her enamell'd skin, weed wide enough to wrap a—*" Mr. O strode into the small space and started when he noticed Trish and me. His silver hair seemed to glow under the fluorescent kitchen lights.

"Ah, we have guests." He bowed to us like we were royalty instead of Little League kids.

"Hi, Mr. O," I said. "He's the owner," I whispered to Trish. Lately half the town seemed to be talking like Abhi when he was at his most theatrical.

"Nice to meet you, Mr. O," Trish said. "Luna's been helping us with a special order for our team."

Mr. O beamed. "Yes, our baseball team, in the championship game. How utterly thrilling!"

"We're playing our toughest rivals," Trish said.

"With our snacks, I'm sure you will prevail," said Mr. O, winking in a conspiratorial way. "Right, Luna?"

Luna nodded stiffly. She seemed freaked out, but I couldn't

figure out why. Mr. O obviously knew we were getting Salt Shaker snacks.

Then I saw it.

Luna was hiding the math book behind her back like she didn't want Mr. O to see it. But why in the world would he care?

"I've just thought of something else to give you," said Luna. "I'll be right back."

She hurried out of the room again as Trish and I stood there awkwardly.

"We love your food," Trish said, oblivious to the fact that our magical math book had left the room.

"We have the best Sports Crisps in the country," Mr. O boasted. "In the world!"

"As far as I know, you have the *only* Sports Crisps anywhere," I said distractedly. Where was Luna? Where was my book?

"Exactly. Our products are unique, and necessary. They are not just empty calories, unlike some bakeries I know of."

"Are you talking about the While Away Café? I don't really like sweets, but their stuff is pretty good," Trish said.

"Exactly, young woman. Sweet treats are not necessary. Not at all. If only some people would understand that once and for all."

Trish furrowed her brow.

"Here we are," Luna said, bringing four more bags into the

room. "These are for your opponents. It won't hurt to foster goodwill between your teams, even if you are rivals on the field."

"What a great idea." Trish grinned. "I can carry these. Ben, are you done packing up?"

I nodded numbly. "So, Luna—" I began.

"I'm sorry, but I must attend to something urgent," said Luna. She turned to Mr. O. "Robin is never here, so I have to do twice the work," she said.

"Is that so? Robin says he's been spending hours at the store," said Mr. O, arching an eyebrow.

"Boys? Has anyone seen Robin today? Or even this week?" Luna asked.

All the Salt Shaker employees in the room shook their heads.

"Come with me, Mr. O, and you can ask the others yourself," said Luna. "Trish and Ben, best of luck in the championship game. Don't forget to share!" She took Mr. O by the arm and they left the kitchen.

I stood rooted to the spot.

"Come on, Ben, let's get going. Let's try to get these to everyone while the fries are still hot."

"She took it," I whispered.

"What?"

"Luna took my math book!" I whispered more vehemently.

Trish shrugged. "Oh, she probably just forgot she was holding it. We can get it later."

"I told you, it's magic!" I realized I was raising my voice. "We need it for the game," I said more calmly.

"That's ridiculous, Ben. Besides, we still have mine at my house. We're stuck on the same puzzle, remember?"

The Salt Shaker employees glanced over their shoulders at us. We couldn't stand here all day.

"Let's go." Trish grabbed her sports bag and the extra snacks.

I picked up my stuff and reluctantly trudged after her.

We had lost the math book. We hadn't been able to solve the latest puzzle.

My stomach sank as we made our way down the street to Sanjay's car.

There was no way we were winning this game.

Chapter Twenty-Three

Trish

Sportsmanship

"It's going to be fine," I reassured Ben as we arrived at the Bridgeton field and made our way to the dugout.

Ben jammed his uniform cap down further on his head. "I've got a bad feeling about this." He fiddled with the laces on his glove.

"Ben," I said. "That math book is fun, but it didn't make you a better baseball player. Things just don't work that way. Mine didn't make me play better, that's for sure."

"The math book made me into a baseball superstar. And as for you . . . I think you started struggling just when you got to the puzzle you couldn't solve."

I blinked. "That was just a coincidence." It wasn't proof that the math book was *magic*. Magic and luck weren't real.

"We have to win. But now I don't think we can," Ben said in a hollow voice.

It was a scorching summer day, and we worked up a sweat as we walked. As we passed the stands, Mom waved to me. She'd finally made it to another game, and I wanted to show her why baseball meant so much to me. I wanted her to see us win.

I took a breath and squared my shoulders. I was with my friends on a great team, and no matter what happened, nothing would change that.

And math puzzle books had nothing to do with playing baseball.

We put down the snacks, and the guys gathered around to grab theirs.

Ben went rapidly to pieces.

He paced back and forth, kicking gloves out of the way and scowling at anyone who got near him. He muttered under his breath, and I had a feeling he was reciting primes to himself. All the confidence and ease he'd displayed over the past couple weeks had evaporated in the time it took to pick up our snacks and come to the ballpark.

Abhi recognized it, too. He came up to me looking concerned.

"What happened to Ben?" he asked.

"He lost his math puzzle book," I said. "He thinks it's the reason why he's been so great at baseball. Because it's . . . magic."

"Well, we still have *your* magic math book," Abhi said.

I rolled my eyes. "That isn't comforting Ben."

Abhi gestured at Ben stomping around the dugout and raised an eyebrow. "We have to get him to calm down."

But Ben wasn't about to stop freaking out.

"Just flip your lucky coin," Abhi said in a soothing voice. "Flip it and see what happens."

Ben dug in his pocket, flipped the coin, and caught it. "Tails." He took off his cap and ran his hand up and down the back of his head.

He flipped the coin again.

"Tails again," said Ben. "See? We're doomed."

"There's nothing ominous about two tails in a row," I said. "According to the laws of probability, you have a fifty percent chance each time you flip the coin, so there's a twenty-five percent chance that it's tails twice in a row."

Ben gave me a look like he was sorry for me and flipped his coin ten more times.

It turned up tails every single time.

Ben paled, and I worried he was going to faint.

I had to stop him before he completely lost it. "Okay, let's not flip the coin anymore," I said. "There must be something stuck to one side that's throwing its weight off."

"There's nothing wrong with my coin. I lost the math puzzle book, and we haven't solved that last puzzle, and our luck has changed!" Ben twisted his cap in his hands like he was trying to shape it into something new.

"Listen," I said. "We can't let this affect us. So what if the coin comes up tails?"

"We're going to lose," Ben moaned softly.

"Stop it!" I said in a loud whisper. "We are an awesome team. Ben, you're about to win MVP!"

Ben jammed the cap back on his head. "Not anymore, I'm not," he said.

I turned to Abhi. "Tell him. It's going to be tough, but you can't seriously believe we have no shot," I said. "We beat the Camemberts in our last game of the season."

"But the coin . . . that's so weird," said Abhi.

That was it. I'd had enough. I wasn't going to let them fall apart like this, not right before our championship game.

"You are *not* going to tell the rest of the team anything about this. Listen to me. Luck does not determine whether we are going to win this game! *We* determine it. With our heads and our hearts and our muscles. We've worked all summer for this chance, and we are not going to throw it away because of some stupid book or a stupid coin."

Ben was still pale, but he nodded shakily. He shoved the coin back in his pocket. Abhi nodded, too.

"Primes," I said, holding out my hand.

"Primes," they repeated, putting their hands on mine.

We were going to play well, and we were going to do our best to win. That was that.

I went to the Camemberts' dugout to deliver their snacks.

"You're in the wrong place," came a deep voice. It was Gigantic Unibrowed Pitcher #1.

"I'm just bringing you guys some snacks," I said.

He glowered at me from under his shaggy unibrow. "Why?"

"To wish you good luck."

He stared at me suspiciously.

"You know, in the spirit of good sportsmanship," I said.

He said nothing.

I sighed. "I'll leave these here. It's chips and fries from the Salt Shaker, the new snack shop in Comity. Take them or leave them, it doesn't matter to me."

He still didn't say anything, so I shook my head and went back to our dugout with a feeling of foreboding.

Chapter Twenty-Four

Ben

The Championship Game

I wanted so badly for Trish to be right.

Our team had found a way to work together and get in sync this summer. Maybe it didn't matter if I didn't have the math puzzler book anymore. Maybe it wouldn't prevent us from beating our archrivals.

We all ate our chips and fries, but they didn't settle well in my stomach, which kept gurgling like a sinister cauldron of anxiety.

Everyone else seemed okay, though. Dad and Coach Deepak conferred with Coach Tom. Campbell whistled as he strolled onto the field to warm up. George pulled up his lucky socks and headed out as well.

But then Garrett swore as he searched through his bag. "Where the heck *are* they?"

"What?" asked Mike.

"My gloves. *My lucky batting gloves,*" said Garrett. "Did you take them out?"

"No way," said Mike, putting his hands on his hips. "We need them to win this game."

"I know!" said Garrett. He scowled and dumped out his bag. He scrambled to sort through the mess—his baseball glove, a sweatshirt, another pair of cleats—but his batting gloves weren't there.

"Oh, no," moaned Abhi.

"What is it now?"

He pointed in front of our dugout.

A black bird sat just outside the baseline.

"A dark portent," said Abhi. "Crows and ravens always signal bad luck in literature. *Come, the croaking raven doth bellow for revenge.*"

I pushed his arm down and begged him to be quiet and not spook the rest of the guys as we came out of the dugout. Every inch of my skin prickled. I went up to the bird and pretended to flap my wings. This usually worked to make a bird fly away.

It flew a few feet, but then landed again and stared at me with a shiny black eye.

I ran toward it, and it flew a few more feet, but then landed and stared again. *I'm not going anywhere*, it seemed to say.

Fine. I was going to ignore it.

"DUCK!" someone cried.

I whirled around to find David fuming and Trish patting the top of her head like she was searching for something.

Coach Tom, Abhi, and I ran over. "What's wrong?"

Trish was breathing rapidly, and her eyes were huge, but she didn't say anything.

David ran up to us. "While Trish was throwing warm-up pitches, a ball came from behind her. If she hadn't ducked, it would have hit her in the head," he said. "You all right?" he asked Trish.

"I'm okay," Trish said shakily.

"Oh, there it is. Thanks, guys." Raccoon Face jogged up with a menacing grin. "We didn't mean to throw it that far. Sometimes we misjudge our strength. Oh, and thanks for the snacks," he said to Trish. "At least Comity's got *one* good thing going for it." He picked up the ball and ran back to his side of the field as we glared at his retreating form.

Coach Tom turned as red as his hair and gritted his teeth. "Are you okay?" he asked Trish.

"Yes, Coach," she said. But she shivered and rubbed her arms.

"I'm going to talk to the ump," said Coach Tom. "Accident, my foot." He stomped off toward the umpire and started yelling as soon as he got within ten feet of him.

The ump yelled back, and five minutes later, Coach Tom

was thrown out of the game. "Joe, Deepak, you guys have got this," he said as he handed Dad his clipboard. "Kids, listen to your coaches, and play your hearts out. I'm proud of you, no matter what. But I'd love it if you beat these . . . these . . ."

He strode away without finishing his sentence.

And there we were, at the start of the championship game of the summer league playoffs with our head coach ejected and our starting pitcher freaked out.

And more black birds had come to join the first one in front of our dugout.

"Ben! Finish your chips," Garrett hissed before the game started.

I reached for my bag of Sports Crisps and stood to walk off some of my jitters.

"No! Sit where you're supposed to sit," said Garrett.

I sighed, took my seat at the end of the bench, and started crunching. The chips were delicious as usual, and my sinuses tingled at their pungent flavor. My stomach gurgled and squeezed. I scanned the crowd and spotted Rob and Mr. O, but didn't see Luna. I was hoping she'd miraculously show up and we'd get the math book back.

The game started off better than expected. Trish led off for us and reached first base with a dribbler down the third base line. But then both Abhi and David struck out. Unibrowed Pitcher #1 smiled and punched his glove as I went up to the plate.

A big meatball, I said to the ball as it left his hand.

But the ball didn't slow down. It didn't glide to me on my command. Without the magic math book, I was back to being useless.

One second, the ball was in the pitcher's hand, and the next, it was in the catcher's glove. It was like I was back at the first game of the summer again.

I shook my head as the jerk on the mound cackled like a hyena.

Dad, at first base, caught my eye and nodded once.

I took a deep breath and faced the next pitch. *Slow down, ball*, I said to myself.

Once again, it landed in the catcher's glove after barely leaving the pitcher's hand. The catcher grunted like a mumbling zombie, and I remembered how much I hated him.

It was time for drastic measures. *Two, three, five*, I thought. *Seven, eleven, thirteen. If you have any pull, Grandma Beth, I'd appreciate it.*

I kept reciting primes to myself as the pitcher released the ball. It didn't slow down. Not a bit.

But I got my bat on it anyway.

I smacked the ball foul, and Trish trotted back to first base and grinned at me.

Seventeen, nineteen, twenty-three, twenty-nine. I prepared for the next pitch.

And when it came, time slowed down. Just a little. It wasn't like before, when the ball seemed so slow I could have plucked it out of the air. There were no sparkles of baseball magic. But the ball was just slow enough that I saw exactly when it floated over the plate. And I smacked it.

It wasn't a home run—I didn't know if I'd ever hit one again without the math book. But it was definitely a hit, a hit that squirted past the shortstop and into the outfield.

Trish rounded second and sprinted to third base while I raced to first.

Now we had two men—well, one man and one woman—on base. I smiled as the pitcher took off his cap and scratched his pointy head. Maybe Trish was right; maybe we didn't need the math book magic to win, just the everyday magic of baseball.

Next up was Garrett. He didn't swing at the first pitch, a wicked curve that started way inside and moved into the strike zone. That was strike one. Then he swung and missed a ball that was way outside. That was strike two.

I took a big lead off first base. With two outs, if Garrett made contact, Trish and I would run as hard as we could.

Garrett fouled off the third pitch, and Trish and I ran back to our bases. He fouled off the next pitch as well, straight back, over the head of the catcher and over the backstop.

The giant pitcher grunted in frustration and wiped his sweaty forehead and unibrow with his sleeve. We were getting in his head!

And then came another pitch. Garrett tapped it just past the shortstop, and I ran like my life depended on it. It kind of felt like it did. Next thing I knew, I'd stopped at second base and found that Trish had scored, and Garrett was standing on first base, grinning.

We were on the board!

But Trish wasn't invincible, and the Camemberts found a way to get hits, too. By the time the fourth inning ended, we were down 3–2.

Trish came up to bat with two outs in the top of the fifth. If we could just score here, we might be able to hold on for one more inning.

She had a great eye. She didn't swing at the first two pitches, which were junk way outside the strike zone. Then she fouled off a scorching fastball right over the plate. The next pitch was inside and low, and Trish stepped back for ball three. The count was 3–1, and Unibrowed Pitcher #1 leaned in for the sign, but shook it off. He looked again, and shook his head again. Behind in the count, what else would he throw but his fastball? He set up and adjusted his grip on the ball. He couldn't be thinking about throwing a curve, could he?

Trish looked like she thought the same thing, because as the ball was released, her eyes widened and she started to swing. But instead of a curve moving out over the plate, it was a fastball way inside. So far inside that there was no time for

Trish to get out of its way. She twisted her body, but the ball hit her left arm with a cracking sound and Trish collapsed to the ground.

The dugout emptied and everyone crowded around.

Trish held her left elbow and rocked back and forth in pain as her dad crouched near her.

Eventually she stood up and let her dad lead her back to the dugout. I could see Trish's mom in the stands, looking pale and stunned. But I caught the shake of the head from Trish's dad, and although she appeared to be itching to come to the dugout, she stayed put.

I followed Trish and her dad into the dugout. The ball had struck Trish just above the elbow, and the area was swelling rapidly and turning a nasty purple.

"We should take you to the ER," said Coach Deepak. "Your arm might be broken."

Trish shook her head. "It's the last game of the summer. It might be my last game ever. Please don't make me go. Even if I can't play, I want to be with my team."

Last game ever? A surge of shock ran through me. Why would Trish quit baseball? Was she moving again? I opened my mouth to ask, but was interrupted by a commotion on the field.

"Let's see how you like getting hit!" bellowed Garrett. He charged the mound and shoved the pitcher, who was easily double his size. Mike, David, and the entire sixth grade contingent backed him up. Then the Camemberts ran up to join the fray.

Abhi, Dad, and I tried to stop the fight erupting on the mound. After some shoving and pulling people apart, we seemed to get things under control.

But when we turned around, Coach Deepak was yelling at the umpire.

"That was what Tom was talking about before the game started! That pitcher might have broken my daughter's arm!" said Coach. "He should be ejected!"

The umpire put his hands on his hips. "It was his first time hitting a batter," he said.

"It was clearly intentional!"

"That's it. You're out!" cried the ump.

Coach Deepak threw his hands up in disgust and stalked to the dugout. "Sorry, Joe," he told Dad. "You better believe I'm complaining to the league about this." And then he left.

Dad was the only coach left. My stomach dropped, and my head started to throb. Would he make all the wrong choices again? Would this game end in disaster, too?

Since Trish had swung at the ball, it was technically a strike despite the fact that she'd been hit. A sixth grader came off the bench to finish the at-bat in her place, but he popped out on the next pitch. That was the end of our chance to score in the top of the fifth.

I was terrified that Dad would try to make me pitch in the

bottom of the fifth, but he showed surprisingly good judgment and chose Abhi instead. The Camemberts, who seemed strangely exhausted and confused at the plate, weren't able to score against him.

So we entered the top of the sixth and final inning still down 3–2. I would be the third batter—possibly the last batter—for my team, just like I'd been in my last championship game two years earlier. We'd lost two of our coaches and our best pitcher, but we could still win if everything went right. But my coin had turned up tails *twelve times in a row.* There was a less than 0.02 percent chance of that happening randomly. Luck, or magic, or whatever we wanted to call it, were against us.

Trish slumped back on the bench with an ice pack pressed to her arm. Fib escaped Mom and ran into the dugout, where he climbed into Trish's lap and laid his head in the crook of her elbow.

It was like he was consoling us ahead of time, trying to make us feel better when we lost.

Chapter Twenty-Five

Trish
The Endgame

I sat fuming in the dugout with a lapful of dog. Fib's weight was the only thing preventing me from pacing the floor. We couldn't lose now, not after everything the Camemberts had put us through. Not after they'd taunted us, bullied us, and injured us. We had some of our best players coming up to bat, though, so we had a great shot at making something happen.

Abhi led off for us. The first pitch blew right by him for strike one.

Garrett, sitting next to me on the bench, let out a small grunt.

Pitch two came in at Abhi's ankles, and he held off swinging to take ball one. "Good eye, Abhi!" I called. Our dugout cheered and the Comity fans in the stands called their encouragement. Aadya and Asha chanted Abhi's name, and Abhi's mom clapped. I searched the stands, but I didn't see

Abhi's dad. He hadn't come to a single game this season, but how could he miss the championship game? Even my mom was at the game. It was too bad she came to a game where I was injured, though.

The pitcher took a long time, shaking off several signs. The catcher called time and visited the mound, where they had a discussion that seemed to take weeks. They were obviously trying to make Abhi nervous, but it wasn't working. He just tugged on his batting gloves and took some practice swings. A warm sensation bubbled up in my chest. Abhi was such an awesome player and friend.

Pitch three looked good, and Abhi fouled it off for strike two. Then came two more balls, which meant he had a full count: three balls, two strikes. I held my breath for the next pitch.

Abhi swung and missed for strike three, but the ball dove down into the dirt and got past the catcher. A wild pitch! Our whole team roared as Abhi sprinted to first base. We had the tying run on base with no outs.

The pitcher, sweating like a beast, spat on the mound and mopped his face with the bottom of his shirt. The catcher, also pouring with sweat, called time and went to confer again as David stepped up to the plate.

The first pitch came in fast, high, and way too close to David's head, but he stepped back quickly and didn't get hit. That pitcher was really trying to hurt us! The crowd murmured; they could see the kind of dirty game Bridgeton was playing, but the ump didn't say a word. Ball one.

Next came a swinging strike. But Abhi sprinted to second before the catcher had a chance to try to throw him out. A fantastic steal! The tying run was on second base with no outs! Then David hit a dribbler down the first base line, and although he was out at first base, Abhi got to third before he could be thrown out.

The tying run was on third with one out and Ben stepping up to the plate.

The pitcher was in bad shape, pale and shaky. Good. They should be scared of us now. A single could tie the game. I didn't believe in luck, but I crossed my fingers (and my toes). The Camemberts were the home team, and if we couldn't tie the game this inning, they would win.

Ben looked around and fidgeted. I wondered if he was thinking about the championship game two years ago, when he was the last batter and his team lost. I hoped he wasn't. He needed to believe in himself like I believed in him.

The pitcher mopped his face again, and his hands trembled.

Then he threw three balls in a row, pitches that were so clearly out of the strike zone that Ben didn't bother to swing. Our fans cheered. The Camemberts coach called time, and the coaches and catcher converged at the mound.

Just like that, the gigantic pitcher was out of the game. The Bridgeton fans cheered for him as he left, and a slightly less gigantic unibrowed pitcher, who could only be his brother, started warming up.

Now that he was ahead in the count, Ben looked more confident as he took his practice swings. I bet he was calculating all the ways he could get a hit and tie the game.

The new pitcher was sweating already, too. He mopped his brow, wound up, and threw.

Ben fouled it back for strike one.

The pitcher swallowed and grimaced. He wound up and threw again.

That pitch was a fastball that Ben tipped for another strike. Full count, three balls and two strikes.

There was no time to talk to Ben. I didn't believe the math books were magic, but they did give me good advice. *Show a sign*: I spun the friendship bracelet on my wrist. *Make it fun*: I willed Ben to remember that this was just a game, and no matter what happened, we'd all still be friends. *Tell the truth*: I had to admit to myself that I wanted us to win. I wanted it more than anything.

I stroked Fib's fur, soft and reddish-brown, and wished with all my might.

Chapter Twenty-Six

Ben

Hurling

Before I stepped in the batter's box again, I caught Abhi's eye as he stood on third base. He gave me a grin and a nod. *You can do it*, he seemed to say. My best friend and I had a shot to keep us in this game. We wouldn't let the team down.

Right over the plate, I whispered to myself.

The pitcher let out a disgusting belch and looked a little green. The pressure was really getting to him. He wound up and threw again.

I'd lost my magic math book, and my lucky coin had said our number was up. But a charge of electricity ran up my arms. As soon as I hit that ball, I knew it was gone.

There were no green sparkles, but it sure felt like magic.

As I rounded first base, basking in the cheers of the crowd, I turned and saw Abhi arrive at home plate. He stepped on the plate, and with that, we had tied the game.

And then the hulking catcher projectile-vomited pink mush all over home plate, narrowly missing Abhi's right foot.

Abhi froze in horror and disgust and gagged, but he didn't vomit. The umpire, too close for comfort, wasn't that lucky. He turned to one side, tore off his mask, and hurled away. Abhi sprang out of the way and sprinted for our dugout.

Next, the pitcher clutched his stomach and threw up on the mound. I pinched my nose shut and tried not to look.

But it didn't make much difference where I looked, since every one of the Camemberts started vomiting. I heard the first baseman splatter the ground behind me, and the second baseman spewed just as I jogged up to him. I dodged around him, tagged second base with my toe, passed the green-faced shortstop, and then moved on to third base, which was already covered in nastiness. The third baseman was doubled over and clutching his stomach.

I held my breath as I navigated a gauntlet of stomach contents.

The fans weren't faring much better. Groans and gagging noises emanated from the stands. Mr. O had a sour look on his face as he led Rob out of the stands and off toward the parking lot. Where were they going?

When I finally arrived at home plate, I did my best to avoid the pile of vomit sprayed on the dirt like the most disgusting abstract painting ever seen. I glanced at the Bridgeton dugout and quickly turned away; everyone in there, including the coaches, was retching, gagging, and worse.

Our dugout had emptied and our entire team was screaming their heads off. Dad squeezed me tight in a hug, and all the guilt I'd been carrying about our last championship game finally melted away.

We had a one-run lead. Because of *me*. But would we be able to finish the game, given the Camemberts' sudden vomit fest?

Once he stopped hurling, the ump called a time-out and made his way to the Camemberts' coaches, who seemed to have recovered as well. He waved Dad over, and as Dad walked there, he rubbed his chest again.

The ump and the coaches talked for a few minutes, and the retching in the other team's dugout calmed down. The players appeared disgusted but less sick than before. One player's mom came over and handed them a roll of paper towels to help them clean up.

After a while, Dad came back to our dugout.

"Is the game over?" I asked.

He shook his head. "Believe it or not, they want to keep playing. They said they just want to wash off, and then they want to finish the game."

After a fifteen-minute delay, the Camemberts were ready to go again. And then their pitcher struck out our next two batters.

We were going to the bottom of the sixth with a lead, and all we had to do was hold on.

Chapter Twenty-Seven

Trish

Moths and Magic

We just needed three more outs. Three outs stood between us and winning the championship, between us and getting to meet the Turkeys, between us and showing the Bridgeton Camemberts once and for all that we were the better team.

Ben held out his hand, and I put mine on it, then Abhi laid his on mine. "Primes," we said together.

Abhi went to the mound to warm up. He looked centered and strong. He was ready.

Ben headed to first base. I shivered as the black birds cawed to each other on the sideline. They might not be a bad omen, but they sure were creepy.

And then, right before Abhi threw his first pitch of the inning, I saw something else, something that made me catch my breath in wonder. Dozens of fluttering dancers spun in the air before me, pale green and spotted. They moved in a spiral, then disappeared into the summer air.

"Moths," I said to myself. But it was still broad daylight, and moths normally flew at night.

"What's up, Trish? Need more ice?" Coach Joe asked.

"I'm fine, Coach, thanks."

But I couldn't help wondering: Why were the moths out so early? Did it mean something? Could this strange game get even stranger?

Abhi threw his first pitch, a wicked fastball. The player Ben called Brick Wall swung and missed. Strike one.

Abhi's second pitch was a breaking ball on the outside of the plate. The batter hit it weakly, and it sailed straight to first base and into Ben's waiting glove. One out!

Next up was Raccoon Face. He took his practice swings, and he seemed to be back to full strength, the bizarre vomiting episode forgotten. Abhi threw another fastball, and Raccoon Face fouled it just outside the first base line, temporarily scattering a few of the black birds. Strike one.

Then came another fastball, and another foul. Strike two.

I hugged Fib closer and let the warmth from his soft fur flow through me. We were going to do it. We had to! Fib's chin felt good against my injured arm—it had stopped throbbing.

Abhi threw again, and the batter knocked the ball down the first base line for a base hit.

Now the tying run was on first, and we only had one out.

Then Abhi faced the next batter, Gigantic Unibrowed Pitcher #2. The one who'd just given up a two-run home run to Ben.

The batter hit the first pitch hard, and my heart leaped into my throat as I watched it fly deep to right field. But Mike caught it and threw it hard to second base to hold the runner on first. It was a textbook play, and now we had two outs.

And then came the next batter—Gigantic Unibrowed Pitcher #1 himself, who loomed larger than ever, and whose pink-splattered baseball pants gave the only hint that he'd very recently been ill. He bared his teeth in a grimace as he swung his huge bat.

My fingers twitched, and I wished I could be out there on the mound with the chance to win the game for our team. I shifted my arm, found green dust from Fib's face all over it, and brushed it off. The swelling on my elbow had gone way down, and it barely ached.

Coach Joe called time and went with our catcher David to talk to Abhi on the mound. After a few moments, they waved Ben over.

What was going on?

But after another couple of moments, Ben returned to first base, and Abhi got ready to pitch again. As he started his windup, I thought about the pink hair, the sneezing fits, the furry donkey hair, the moths, and now, this sudden vomiting, all short-lived but disruptive, and I wondered what could have caused them all. Was it really magic? Great, now I was thinking like Ben.

Baseball is magic. Time stops between the instant the ball is released and when it makes it over the plate, between the whack of the bat and when the ball finally touches earth again. The next few moments passed in front of my eyes like a slow-motion movie.

Abhi threw his pitch, and the ball flew toward the batter.

The batter brought his bat back and began to move it forward.

Abhi turned his head to look at something along the first base line. He smiled and started to raise his glove.

The ball pinged against the bat and sped back toward the mound.

Chapter Twenty-Eight

Ben

Baseball and Broken Hearts

Dad was the only coach left. When he went to the mound to talk to Abhi, I was so nervous that he'd made up his mind about what he wanted to do, and that nothing or no one could convince him otherwise.

Then he called me over.

"You guys are the ones who've been playing," Dad said to Abhi, David, and me. "And you held your own practices last week without the coaches around. I wanted to make the batter sweat a little. But while we're here, what's your strategy?"

My mouth fell open. He wasn't telling us what we should do. He didn't tell us how to stand, or catch, or pitch. He was *asking* us.

Abhi and David talked about the pitches they wanted to use. I just nodded. Dad listened and nodded, too. But he was rubbing his chest again like something was bothering him.

I returned to first base, but my eyes kept darting to our dugout. Had Grandma Beth done the same thing in that last championship game? I couldn't remember.

Baseball's full of numbers. And right now, all the numbers seemed to be counting down to something important, maybe even momentous.

Five—the number of innings we'd finished playing.

Four—the number of puzzles we'd solved in my copy of *The Mathematics of The Wild* before it got taken away.

Three—the number of "Primes" on our team—Abhi, Trish, and me.

Two—the number of years I'd stayed away from baseball.

One—the number of dads I had.

Abhi wound up. *Say it out loud*: "Let us win," I whispered to myself. *Show you care*: Had I shown Dad? Not really. *Reveal what's in your heart*: "Just let Dad be okay, and I'll tell him," I murmured. All the things I hadn't said crowded into my head.

I talked to the ball as Abhi let go. *Go faster, move outside*, I said. I wanted this batter to miss, and miss big. But there were no green sparkles as the ball raced toward the batter.

I saw the bat make contact, heard the ping of the hit. The ball flew like an arrow toward Abhi, coming back even faster than he'd thrown it.

Abhi was a pitcher. He was used to catching line drives like that at point-blank range. But he didn't get a glove on this ball.

It hit him, and he dropped like a stone.

I ran to the mound.

Abhi's eyes were closed. He wasn't talking or moving.

"Abhi!" I said. "Dude, what's wrong?" I shook him, but he didn't respond.

Dad and Trish arrived at the same time as Trish's mom, Dr. Das. She felt Abhi's neck. "Call 911 and tell someone to get the AED," she said. Then she started pushing on Abhi's chest, starting CPR.

What?

"Hurry," she said to Dad in a voice that was shockingly calm.

Then came a blur of activity. The kit arrived, and Dr. Das attached pads to Abhi's chest, told everyone to step back, and zapped Abhi with the machine. The *defibrillator.* She pushed a button, and my best friend's body convulsed like a doll. She felt his neck again, and went back to CPR.

I couldn't believe what I was seeing. *Abhi!*

Dr. Das pressed the button again, and it seemed to work—she stopped doing CPR—but she wouldn't let anyone else get close to Abhi.

Next thing I knew, Abhi was strapped to a stretcher, given an oxygen mask, and whisked away in an ambulance. Abhi's dad climbed into the ambulance with him (when had he shown up to the game?), and his mom and the twins followed in their car.

People stayed for a bit in stunned silence, but the game was over. No one cared who won. The Bridgeton batter stammered his apology to anyone who would listen.

"I was just trying to get a hit," he said. "I didn't mean to hit *him.*"

I couldn't stand that guy or his team, but I felt sorry for him. I knew what it was like to hurt someone without meaning to. "It wasn't your fault," I said.

Which was true. It was mine.

The thought kept repeating like a heartbeat in my head: *My fault. My fault. My fault.*

I couldn't solve that last math puzzle. I'd let Luna take away the book. If I'd had the book and solved the puzzle, maybe I could have talked that ball away from Abhi. Instead, it had zoomed back at him like lightning.

"It hit him in the chest," Dr. Das said. "A one in a million chance, but sometimes it happens. And it was hit hard enough to stop his heart."

Stop his heart! Abhi was my best friend. *My fault. My fault.*

"Will he be okay?" asked Trish in a shaky voice.

"He has a great chance," said her mom. "He's in good hands now."

People trickled away from the field in dribs and drabs.

Parents gathered up their kids and hugged them, and then they went home.

And to think we'd started the afternoon worried about who would win a baseball game.

Grandma Beth had been right. Baseball is designed to break your heart.

Chapter Twenty-Nine

Trish

The Final Puzzle

"He's going to be okay," I whispered to Ben. "Mom will make sure of it." We were in the parking lot of the Bridgeton baseball field, getting ready to drive to our house. Dad had been hovering there trying to catch as much of the game as possible. Once he found out what had happened, he invited Ben's family to our house while Mom went to the hospital to keep an eye on Abhi. For the first time in forever, I was grateful she'd gone there.

Mom had made sure all the fields had AEDs. And she'd been amazing when the worst had happened. Abhi's heart had stopped, but thanks to Mom, he had a shot at being okay.

Ben didn't say anything at first. Then he whispered, almost too low for me to hear, "It's my fault that Abhi got hurt."

"That's ridiculous," I said.

But Ben just shook his head and stared at the pavement.

We got in the backseat of our car and Fib laid across our laps like a warm blanket.

"We've got to do something," Ben whispered.

"What can we do?"

"When we get to your house, go get the math book."

I sighed. There he went again with the magic stuff. But Abhi was terribly injured, and neither of us knew what to do. I wanted to do something, anything to help.

I nodded.

As soon as we arrived, Ben and I raced up to my room. I pulled the book from my nightstand. I smoothed the worn cover. The late-afternoon light made it look ancient. I opened the book and read its odd title again:

The Mathematics of The Wild

"I don't understand how this book can help. Even if it is . . . magical." I said the word carefully. It tasted strange in my mouth. "We don't need help with baseball anymore. How can this help Abhi?"

"It's magic, Trish. It can help us with anything. Especially since it helped cause this problem."

"You said that in the car. What do you mean?"

Ben ran his hands through his hair absently. "I told you the math puzzles made me better at baseball. I didn't tell you exactly how, though." He glanced at me, and I did my best to keep from looking skeptical.

"When I solved the first puzzle, and the words *say it out loud* appeared, I took them literally."

"You already told me this. It's how you solved my puzzle," I said.

"Yeah, but I also started talking to the baseball, telling it what to do. To slow down, or speed up, or swerve into the strike zone."

I forced myself not to roll my eyes. "Yeah, yeah. Baseball magic. You told me."

"And . . . I saw—just stay with me, okay—green sparkles around the ball. That's how I knew that magic was occurring."

"What?" I exclaimed.

"You saw them, too?"

"Never," I said. "Sorry, Ben. There's no such thing as magic. You did this on your own."

Ben swallowed. "I know what happened this summer. If I hadn't lost my math book to Luna . . . if I had just solved that last puzzle, I could have *talked* to that ball and made it swerve so it didn't hit Abhi. Or swerve out of the strike zone so the batter never even hit it. Don't you see?" Ben turned his face away. "It's my fault."

"That was a solid hit, Ben. There was no time for him to react. I don't think it would have been much different even if your . . . magic . . . had been at work. Like Mom said, it was like a one in a million shot, what happened to Abhi. It was just terrible luck."

"I thought you didn't believe in luck," Ben said.

"Maybe I do now. Besides, it's *my* fault Abhi got hurt."

"I can't wait to hear this."

I moved my left arm back and forth and showed him where I'd been hit. There wasn't even a bruise. "I wasn't hurt that badly. I should have stayed in and pitched. Abhi shouldn't have been on the mound."

Ben's eyes grew huge. "How is that possible? I saw your arm. It was wrecked!"

I shrugged my shoulders. "It hurt a lot when I was hit, but I guess it wasn't that bad?"

"There's something weird going on," said Ben. "It's magic. It has to be. We've got to solve this problem, and then maybe we'll understand."

We opened my book and flipped to the baffling puzzle:

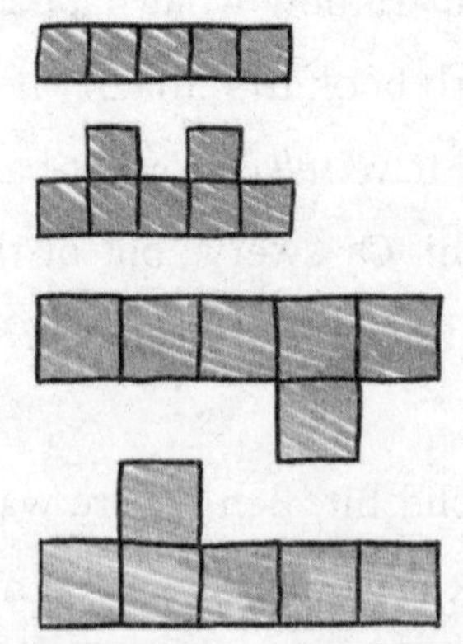

I stared at it. Ben stared at it. I stared at Ben staring at it, and he stared at me.

"Anything?" I asked.

"Nope."

I handed the book to Ben and flopped sideways on my bed. If Ben and I couldn't figure out this answer over the past few weeks, what hope did we have of solving it tonight?

Ben kept looking at it like he had X-ray vision and was trying to see right through it. "Every other puzzle had *numbers*. I have to believe there are numbers in this one, too," he said.

Lying on my side, I glanced at the puzzle, and suddenly something became clear. I shot up. "Ben, give that back for a second."

Ben handed it to me. "You have an idea?"

"I think we might need a different perspective." I took the book and turned it:

"Do you see the numbers now?"

Ben squinted. "Yes!" he said. "The numbers aren't in the colored part, but the spaces in between. And there's a . . . two, I think. And three? Twenty-three? Which is prime!"

"Okay, let's try it." I wrote *23* in the book.

It didn't turn green. It sank into the page and disappeared. "It's not right."

"What do you mean, it's not right? We don't have time for this!" Ben stalked to the window.

I examined the puzzle again. "The three is smaller . . . I wonder . . . do you think it's an exponent? Like, two to the third power?"

"Two times two times two. That's eight. It's not prime," Ben said.

"Yeah, but we should at least try it, right?"

Ben nodded, and I wrote *8* at the bottom of the puzzle.

It turned green!

We had finally solved the puzzle that had stumped us for weeks! But of all the answers we'd found, why was this number not prime?

"Now it's got to tell us how to help Abhi," said Ben. "Come on, book, don't fail us now."

And then a sentence appeared.

What is the ultimate answer?

Chapter Thirty

Ben

The Ultimate Answer

"What does that mean? We solved the puzzle, and now the book's supposed to tell us what to do, not ask us a question!" I said. I couldn't sit a second longer, and stood again to pace the room.

"Let's think about the answers we've found so far," Trish said. "Maybe we need to calculate something using them?"

That was as good an idea as any. I grabbed a piece of paper and wrote what we'd learned so far:

Trish's Book:	Ben's Book:
1	1
5	13
8	2
	3

"I'll do addition and subtraction, and you can try multiplication and division," I said.

We each grabbed pieces of paper and did our calculations.

"Try eleven," I said.

Trish scrawled it on the page. Nothing.

7,800 wasn't right, either. Neither was 33, or 0.0003, or 3,120.

Trish chewed on her knuckle. "I don't see how this would help Abhi."

"It has to. Can I see the book again?" I asked.

Trish handed it to me. If we couldn't solve this, Abhi was on his own. We wouldn't let that happen. I still couldn't shake the guilt that it was my fault he was hurt.

I flipped to the beginning of the book. "This first sudoku-like puzzle. Why is it here?"

She blinked at me. "I don't know. It's just another puzzle, right?"

"There has to be something more to it. All the other puzzles have number solutions, but this one only uses letters. And I had a similar puzzle in my book." There was something familiar about those letters. I began to turn them over in my mind. It was right there . . .

"But this doesn't have anything to do with math." Trish furrowed her brow.

I took the piece of paper and added the extra information:

Trish's Book:	Ben's Book:
1	1
5	13
8	2
First puzzle: RISLAP	3
	First puzzle: SPETLA

"Maybe the letters spell something?"

I took a piece of paper and played around with the letters: SPETLA, PETLAS . . .

PETALS.

"Ben! Look!"

Trish showed me what she'd written. "Mine spells something. SPIRAL."

Fib came in the room, sat in front of us, and put his paw on my knee. I reached down to trace the soft white spiral on his head.

And that's the moment when the numbers flipped into place for me.

"Fib! That's it, Trish! Fibonacci!"

We knew the answer.

My hand shook as I wrote the numbers in the right order: *1, 1, 2, 3, 5, 8, 13.* Each number was the sum of the two before it. It was the Fibonacci sequence, the sequence repeated everywhere in nature. In pine cones, daisies, and sunflowers, as we'd told Rob back at the beginning of the season. In nautilus shells and hurricane spirals.

We sat back and waited for something to happen. The numbers turned green, sank into the page, and disappeared.

And nothing else happened.

"What? I wrote them in the right order." I tried again: *1, 1, 2, 3, 5, 8, 13.*

The numbers turned green and disappeared, but that was it. No sentence, no solution, no cure for Abhi.

"What's wrong? Why isn't it working?" I shook the book in frustration.

Trish laid a hand on my arm. "Maybe it just needs a moment."

I thought to myself that the book had never "needed time" before, but you never knew. I took deep breaths and walked to the other side of the room, then walked back slowly.

"Did anything happen?" I asked as I peered over Trish's shoulder.

She shook her head.

"What is the ultimate answer? We've got to find it, to find a way to save Abhi." My voice cracked, and I choked back a sob.

Trish swiped a tear from her face. "He's my friend, too. We'll find the answer. We're so close, I can feel it." She chewed on her lip and flipped through the book again. "We must be missing something."

"But what?" I said.

"Well, except for the first one, the solutions to all the other puzzles were single numbers. Maybe we have to choose just one?"

I shook my head. "That doesn't make any sense. Why did we have to figure all the others out, then?"

"Maybe *one*? Because it's repeated?"

We tried.

The *one* didn't turn green. It disappeared.

I put my face in my hands. "It's over. Nothing's going to work. Nothing's going to help Abhi. Our math skills are failing us just when we need them the most. Our baseball team pulled together, but everything's still falling apart. What if Abhi is never the same again?"

"Let me have the book a second," Trish said.

She smoothed the page. She took a pen and wrote:

Phi. The golden ratio, the proportion that the Fibonacci numbers approached. The ratio that was repeated over and over again in nature.

The symbol turned bright green. I held my breath and waited. A sentence appeared:

Here you will find what you seek. Bring the key.

We turned the page and found a map with a glowing green circle at one end. "What is it?" Trish asked.

I studied the map for a moment, then looked up at Trish. "It's a map of the Comity Woods. I think we need to find something in that circle."

"I can't believe this is happening," said Trish. "Who is doing this? Who gave us this book?"

"I'm pretty sure it's Rob," I said.

"Rob? What makes you think that?"

"Well—"

There was a knock on the door, and Sanjay poked his head in. "Come down for dinner. Mom's supposed to call soon to update us on what's going on with Abhi."

We went downstairs, and Trish's mom called while we were snarfing dinner from Pizza Napoli. Her dad answered the phone and spoke with her for a few minutes while we all hung on his every word, trying to figure out what was happening.

He finally hung up. "Abhi's stable. He's awake and with his family. But he's in the ICU, and they're going to need to observe him, because there's some heart damage."

"Heart damage? How bad is it?" I asked.

"His heart was bruised by the impact of the ball. They're going to monitor him to see whether it gets better with time."

"You mean there's a chance he won't recover?" Trish asked with a hitch in her voice.

Trish's dad ran his hands over his eyes. "The doctors are taking great care of him. I hope he comes home soon, healthy as ever."

But Trish and I were determined to do much more than hope.

Chapter Thirty-One

Trish

The Fountain

Mom returned to the hospital early the next morning to check on Abhi. She texted an update: *HE'S ABOUT THE SAME. HE'S STILL IN THE ICU, SO NO ONE BUT FAMILY CAN VISIT. I'LL LET YOU KNOW IF ANYTHING CHANGES.*

Right after that, I begged Sanjay to drop me off at Ben's house. I'd stowed the math book in my backpack; maybe the book itself was the *key* that the map mentioned?

I found Ben in his kitchen, scratching Fib behind the ears. "Sorry, boy," he said. "I don't know how long we'll be gone, so you need to stay put." We stepped outside, and Ben closed the door on Fib's sad furry face. We followed the path from Ben's yard into the woods and followed the map, hoping to find the glowing green circle quickly.

But after hours of walking, we had traveled to Bailey Park

and the other end of the Comity Woods, but never made it anywhere near anything like a glowing green circle. In fact, we never went anywhere that Ben hadn't been dozens of times before.

"Where is that giant tree?" he asked. "The one where you ended up after the last game of the season?"

I shrugged my shoulders. "I don't know how I got there. I was just trying to get lost," I said. "Eventually, Fib showed up, and that's where we ended up."

The map wasn't helping. Eventually, Claudia and Sanjay texted us, and we had to go home.

"We'll get there tomorrow," I said.

But we didn't. And we didn't get there the next day, or the next, or the next. We'd solved the final math puzzle, and all we had to show for it was sore feet.

Abhi was moved out of intensive care, and we were excited to visit him in the hospital and see for ourselves how he was doing. But although we tried to see him on two different afternoons, he was away from his room for hours both times, off doing tests the doctors had ordered. Each time, we were forced to leave when we reached the end of visiting hours. We left him notes, but it was frustrating not to be able to see him.

"He's better," Mom said. "He just needs time to heal." But the worry line appeared between her eyes.

If I believed in luck, I would have sworn that it had turned against us, that there was something preventing us from seeing Abhi, just like it was preventing us from getting to the spot marked on the map in *The Mathematics of The Wild*.

We had to do something. We had to see where the map led.

The next morning, I got to Ben's house early.

"Where are you two going?" asked Ben's dad.

"Just taking a walk in the woods," said Ben.

"Again? Do me a favor and take Fib this time. He's been going nuts every time you leave without him, and he could use the exercise."

"But—"

Then it hit me. "Sure, Mr. Messina," I said. "We can take him."

Ben gave me a look but shrugged his shoulders and got Fib's leash. Fib took one look and wagged his entire body, and I could swear he was smiling.

We stepped outside. "Why'd you say yes to bringing Fib?" Ben asked.

"Because I think that every time either of us has gone to an unusual part of the woods, Fib has been with us," I said.

Ben's eyes widened, and his mouth made an O of surprise. "The key!" he said.

"Exactly."

We walked through Ben's yard and onto the path that led

to Bailey Park with Fib eagerly leading the way. He strained at his leash, but Ben kept a good hold on him so he couldn't suddenly disappear.

The morning was clear and cool, and the sunlight threw shadows on the path through the woods, shadows in complicated patterns, like a mysterious code that held the answers to everything.

Ben stopped at a branch point where two big evergreens leaned against each other and consulted the map in the math book. I couldn't help feeling anxious about where this adventure would lead. I wondered what we would find, and I hoped it would be what we needed to help Abhi.

"This is where things start getting weird," said Ben.

"*Start* getting weird?" I asked. "What do you call the past few weeks?"

That earned me a nervous smile from Ben. "Ready?" he asked.

We ducked to get under the two shaggy trees and plunged into the deeper woods beyond.

"This has got to be it," Ben said.

"How do you know?" I murmured.

"Because until this summer, I'd never been here before, and I've been running through these woods my whole life."

A chill ran down my spine.

Soon, we started hiking up a steep hill. The trees thinned,

and sunlight lit everything up. There was a refreshing, minty smell in the air, and I took deep breaths, like I'd never get enough.

"Where are we?" I asked.

"Close, I think," said Ben. He pointed at Fib, who seemed even more energized than usual, and was sniffing the ground furiously.

Ben examined the book again, but it was obvious that we didn't need the map anymore. We just had to follow Fib's madly wagging tail.

The sound of running water floated to us long before we came to a rocky outcropping where Fib finally stopped. He tugged the leash out of Ben's hand, ran to the center of the rocks, and leaped over the outer ring, landing with a splash.

"Fib!" called Ben. "Is this it, boy?"

We ran the last few yards, then stopped and watched Fib.

He was swimming in a pool of clear water that seemed to be lit from within by a bright green light. The dog seemed absolutely ecstatic, with shining eyes and a big doggy smile. He paddled around with ease as we approached. And once we got closer, we realized the pool didn't just look green; it was surrounded by a ring of green powder that coated the rocks around it. This was clearly where Fib had picked up the green dust that he'd been smearing over everything.

"Come on, Fib. We've got to look for the magic thing that

can help Abhi. You can swim some other time," Ben said.

"It's so peaceful and dreamy here," I said.

I touched the place on my arm where the pitch had hit me. I thought I'd broken a bone. But here I was, good as new. And that wasn't the only time I'd recovered quickly from an injury. My mind spun as I touched my right wrist, the one that Ben had stepped on.

Both times, I'd wiped green dust from my skin.

"The Fountain of Youth," I whispered.

"What'd you say?"

"Never mind," I said. "Just a silly thought."

"No, you're right." Ben's eyes grew wide. "Fib's found the Fountain of Youth!"

"Ben, you know there's no—"

"There's been magic right in front of us the whole time! Fib licked your wrist after you . . . after I hurt you in our first game," he said. "And it was healed almost immediately!" Ben thought for a moment, then exclaimed, "And my ankle!"

I blinked. "Your ankle?"

"I twisted my ankle when I ran off after the This Is a Stick game. It was really bad, and I could barely make it home. But Fib licked it, and it stopped throbbing, and by the time I woke up the next morning, it was back to normal."

"Maybe . . ." I touched my left arm. It had hurt so terribly when I'd gotten hit, but after Fib put his head on my arm, it stopped. And by the end of the game, it even looked normal. "Do you think the water cures people?"

"Not just people. This explains how Fib's arthritis suddenly disappeared, too. The water, yeah . . . and maybe the green dust, too."

"Do you think it can cure Abhi? Of a bruised heart?"

"Only one way to find out. Hand me your water bottle."

Ben's hands shook as he emptied the water onto the forest floor. "I'll take some water and some of the green dust, too," he said. "It's too bad we don't have more containers."

"How much do you think it will take to help Abhi?" I asked.

"Maybe not just Abhi," Ben said quickly. "It's the Fountain of Youth! Maybe we can help other people, too. Why else would we have gotten the math book? We needed to find the ultimate answer, and now we have."

"Let's focus on Abhi for now," I said. I couldn't shake the nagging feeling that this seemed too easy. Why was Fib the only one who'd ever found this place? Who gave us *The Mathematics of The Wild*, and what did they know about this fountain?

Ben knelt down and prepared to dip the bottle into the green pool.

"Be careful," I said.

Ben laughed. "Fib is swimming around in there. It's not going to hurt me." He dragged the bottle through a shallow area full of green dust, and then sat up and screwed the lid back on the bottle.

"Does it feel funny?" I asked.

"No, it just feels like water. Try it yourself."

I poked a finger and then my whole hand into the water. It appeared green in the sunlight. The water was cool and refreshing, and the worry I'd been carrying around eased. I took a breath and my muscles relaxed.

"Okay, we've got it. Let's get out of here," Ben said. "Fib, come. Let's go home."

Fib lumbered out of the pool, rubbing his entire body in green dust. Once he was on dry ground again, he stood and shook himself, scattering droplets everywhere.

We'd done it! We'd found the place marked in the book. But would it really help Abhi? I guessed there was only one way to know for sure.

Suddenly, Fib started whining. He gave a high-pitched bark.

"Hold it right there!" came a voice from behind us.

Chapter Thirty-Two

Ben

The Price

"If you want to take that, you'll need to pay the price," said Rob, stepping out from the shadow of the trees.

Fib ran to him and jumped on him like he was an old friend.

"I was wondering when you'd show up," I said. "Fib, off!" For once, Fib listened.

Rob raised an eyebrow. "Really?"

I nodded. "Yeah. First, you show up wearing a sparkly green hat and knocking homers like they were ping-pong balls. Then my old dog starts running around like a puppy again. You talk to Trish and me about math, and then a math book shows up at my house. A *magical* math book that made me suddenly amazing at baseball. How many different magical people could there be running around here?"

"Perhaps more than you think," came another voice.

Luna stepped out from the trees, and Fib ran to her and licked her hand.

"What are you doing here?" Rob asked Luna. "Why aren't you at the all-important store?"

"The store should be important to you, too, dear Robin," Luna shot back. "We are supposed to work together, but of the two of us, I'm the only one who works at all."

Trish frowned. "You were the ones I overheard," she said. "The other day, outside the While Away Café."

"I thought it was one of the few places where we could have our discussions in private," said Luna.

"Discussions! That's what you call them? I call them nagging," Rob said darkly.

I rounded on Luna. "Why'd you take my math book?"

She narrowed her eyes and stared me down. "*Your* math book? Ha! *Lord, what fools these mortals be!*"

That kind of talk reminded me of Abhi and made my chest constrict. "Maybe if we'd had it, we would have won the game, and our friend wouldn't be horribly hurt."

Luna drew back. "What are you talking about?"

"Our friend Abhi," Trish said. "He got hit in the chest with a baseball—"

"And now he's in the hospital, and we need to heal him with the water and dust from this fountain," I said.

If looks could kill, the look Luna gave Rob would have incinerated him. "What precisely did you do with our books, dear Robin?"

"Your books?" I asked numbly.

Rob smiled and removed his sparkly baseball cap, shaking his blond curls. "Oh, Luna, they needed them more than we did. This"—he indicated Trish and me—"was my project this summer."

"You handed these young mortals the *Books of Power given to us by our king*, the books we were supposed to use to guarantee our success this summer?"

"Books of Power? King?" What in the world was going on around here?

Trish shushed me. "Is this about the wager?" she asked.

I was getting more and more confused.

"Everything is about the wager. Always," said Rob. "But there are more important things under the summer sky."

"You disobeyed *all* our orders! And yet you are still the chosen one, the right hand of our king," Luna said, her yellow eyes full of venom.

"As I always shall be," Rob said, lifting his chin.

"We don't have time to listen to you two argue," I said. "We need to get this water back to our friend, and we need to go now, to make sure he recovers." I gripped the bottle full of the magic water tightly, took Trish's arm, and tried to get past Rob.

"Sorry about your friend," Rob said smoothly, "but as I said, you cannot take that from here without paying the price."

"What do you want?" I asked.

"Wait a minute," Trish said. "Who are you guys, anyway?"

"Have you not guessed?" Rob asked with a laugh. "You saw us watching the play, did you not?"

"The play? You mean the one my sister was in?" I said. None of this was making sense!

"Yes," said Luna. "The one that never even mentions *me*."

"Why would it mention you?" asked Trish. "It's a story about fairies."

"Exactly," said Rob with a wink and a smile.

Trish snorted. "You can't possibly think we'd believe you two are *fairies*."

"Why not?" asked Luna with a gleam in her eye.

"You're saying . . . that fairies actually exist?" I asked.

"Yes," said Rob. "As much as magic math books and lucky coins."

I opened and closed my mouth, but no sound came out. I knew there was magic in the world, but I'd never imagined fairies who looked like people.

"Fine, you're fairies," Trish said, rolling her eyes and clearly still not believing them. "What do you want from us?"

"We aren't just *any* fairies," said Rob, moving closer.

"We're the lieutenants of King Oberon," said Luna, also moving closer.

"King Oberon?" asked Trish.

"Yes," said Rob. "All those fairies Shakespeare wrote about. King Oberon, Robin Goodfellow, and . . . unnamed helper fairy."

"See? Not even a *mention*," Luna exclaimed.

I held my hands up. "Are you saying you're *fairies from Claudia's play*? Like, those exact ones?" I wished Abhi were here; it would be like all his dreams coming true at once.

"One and the same," said Rob. "Although Will Shakespeare always did like to embellish things a bit."

"Puck, Puck, always Puck!" cried Luna. "*Robin* did this, and *Robin* did that. What about me? Why do I never get credit?"

"I'm just so much more interesting than you, dear Luna," Rob said lazily.

"Stop!" I yelled.

They stopped bickering and turned to me.

"What do you want? We need to get this water to our friend." I paused. "That is, if it will cure him?"

"It should," said Rob. "But there is the simple matter of payment."

Luna nodded. "Every gift from The Wild comes with a price."

Trish reached for my hand. "What do you want?" I asked again.

"See? *They* found a way to get along," said Luna, glaring at Rob. "And they couldn't stand each other at the beginning of the summer."

"That is *my* doing!" Rob cried. "My project has been a success, indeed."

"What do you want?" I yelled. Every heartbeat we spent out here meant more time that Abhi was left to heal alone.

"Ah, yes," said Rob. "That's just it. We just want what belongs to us."

Luna faced me and held out her hand. "The book, please."

I glanced at Trish, and she nodded once. I was reluctant to give up the magical book, but it had to be done. "Here." I handed it to Luna. "Now can we go help our friend?"

Luna and Rob both bowed their heads, and I took that to mean we were free to go. "Come on, Fib," I said. "Let's bring this to Abhi."

"I'm afraid that won't be possible," said a new voice that echoed through the small grove. A voice that sounded like tree branches creaking in the wind.

Fib spooked. He yanked the leash out of my hand and took off into the woods.

Chapter Thirty-Three

Trish

The Heart of the Matter

"No one leaves," said Mr. O. His silver hair gleamed white in the sunlight. "There are some things I must explain."

I froze in my tracks like I'd come up against an invisible barrier. I glanced at Ben, and I could see he couldn't move, either.

We had no choice but to listen.

"The books were for Rob and Luna," said Mr. O. "To get them to work together to solve the problems. If they had done that, they would have received all they needed in order for our enterprise to work, and for us to win the wager."

"Excuse me, Mr. O," I said. "Or should I call you King Oberon?"

"You may address me as King Oberon, I suppose, or the King of The Wild," he said. But then his eyes crinkled. "But I prefer Mr. O."

"Okay. Mr. O, then. Why would fairies need the Fountain of Youth?"

"Smart girl." Mr. O brought his hands together and steepled his fingers. "The Books of Power would not have led Robin and Luna here. They act to help their users solve whatever challenges they face. If you solve the Book's puzzle, it will aid you in your quest, whatever it is."

"See?" said Ben. "I told you it was magic."

"Fine," I said. I addressed Mr. O again. "What exactly is this wager that seems to be at the heart of all the strange things that have been going on this summer?"

His smile was as sharp as a knife. "It is the Midsummer's Wager, a most ancient tradition. Each summer, my royal wife and I have a . . . friendly competition. And this year, we are here in this town of Comity, wagering on food."

Something clicked in my head. "Your wife—Queen Titania—she runs the While Away Café, right?"

"That is correct," said Mr. O. "And although she started off at a disadvantage, she quickly recovered her stride and has given us real competition."

"So if I understand right," Ben said, scratching his head, "a bunch of fairies are in our town, and the thing they're doing is *creating competing restaurants*?"

"Indeed. My royal queen loves sugar, but I know it is useless, empty. Salt is always superior. Salt from the oceans, salt that runs in the veins of every living thing."

I wasn't a fan of sweets, but this was a bit extreme.

"You're arguing about whether savory treats or sweet ones are the best?" Ben laughed incredulously.

But Mr. O nodded seriously. "And the stakes are high: Whoever loses is banished from the town of Comity for two hundred years. That's more than two lifetimes for humans! If the While Away wins, you mortals must continue to settle for success in literature and music. But if the Salt Shaker wins, just imagine: Comity would be a town where science, mathematics, and sports of all kinds would flourish for two centuries. Wouldn't that be marvelous?"

Why did we have to choose? "I think it would be great if all those things were here," I said, and Ben nodded.

But Mr. O wasn't listening. "In order to win, we at the Salt Shaker have needed to work together as a team, which, alas, we have not."

"Through no fault of mine, my king!" cried Luna. "Robin has not lifted a finger, while I've been working day and night to help us win."

"I've been doing my part in my own way," said Robin. "Why do you think any of the local sports teams believe that our snacks would help them perform? Who do you think came up with the product names?"

"You can't eat a name," said Luna, her yellow eyes flashing. "Who's been working away, developing recipes? Who's been keeping operations running smoothly?"

"This is exactly why I gave you two those Books. You would have done better doing your own work, rather than foisting it onto these mortals."

"Robin did it, my king, not me," said Luna.

"I took her book away for three days before she even noticed it was missing," said Rob.

"The fault is in you both." Mr. O turned to Ben and me. "Tell me, young ones, what did you learn from the Books?"

"Well, the puzzles were hard, but if you put them all together, they formed the Fibonacci sequence," I said.

"So we put the numbers in order," said Ben. "But that wasn't really the answer."

"The answer was Phi," I said. "And then we found the path that led us here, to the magic fountain. The Fountain of Youth."

Oberon nodded. "But what is the ultimate answer?"

"Like Trish said, it's Phi," Ben said.

"Which is?" Mr. O was being maddening.

"1.618," I said. "But it's an irrational number, a number that goes on and on, never ending and never repeating."

Mr. O shook his head. "The answer is not a *number*," he said.

"But that's what Phi is!" Ben cried. "It's a number, okay? A number related to the Fibonacci sequence, which is found over and over in nature. That's why it's a fairy number, I guess."

"It is not a number of which I speak," said Mr. O. His eyes were gray and flashed oddly. "It is something else. Something that Robin and Luna would do well to understand. That was my intention, when I wrote the puzzles."

"*You* wrote them?" I asked, surprised.

"Of course. Because they needed to learn a lesson, if we were ever to succeed."

I frowned. I had no idea what he was getting at, and from the expression on Ben's face, neither did he.

"It is not the numbers in and of themselves that are important," said Mr. O.

It finally dawned on me what Mr. O was driving at. "That's it!" I said. I turned to Ben in excitement. "It's not the numbers. Remember what your mom said, Ben?"

"It's the ratio between them," Ben said.

"Phi, not primes," I said. "Petals and leaves are arranged in Fibonacci spirals so each one gets the best share of the sun."

"And I guess that's what friendship is about, too. And being in a family. Arranging things so they're best for the group, and not just for one person," Ben said.

"And that goes for baseball teams, and math teams, too. Any team," I said.

"Precisely, my young friends. Precisely," said Mr. O. "That is what I was hoping that Luna and Robin would discover together. So they could become friends and partners, not rivals. And then we just might start winning the Midsummer's Wager again. We have lost so many times, despite always being more organized than my dear queen's entourage."

"We should have listened to you, oh King of The Wild," said Rob. He knelt.

"Worry not, dear Robin," said Mr. O. "We still have time this summer to turn the tide. Now, dear Robin, dear Luna, we should go to the store, and set things aright. There are already rumors spreading through the town about the commotion during the championship game."

"You mean, people are saying you're the reason Abhi got hurt?" Ben asked.

Luna raised her eyebrows. "Of course not. They are wondering who poisoned your opponents."

"Poisoned?" I asked.

"Already, word is spreading that someone cheated to help your team try to win."

"Well, you can just tell them it isn't true!" Ben shouted. "There's been all kinds of weird stuff happening this summer as the result of your snacks."

"Yeah," I said. "Hair turning strange colors, and sneezing fits, and furry hair like a donkey's," I said.

"It must be sabotage from the While Away," said Luna. "Those dessert lovers may seem sweet, but they will stop at nothing to win."

"Too true, too true," said Mr. O. "My royal wife has never gotten over that incident with Bottom."

My head was spinning. "That actually happened? You made your own wife fall in love with a donkey-headed man?"

"Anything to win," said Mr. O, his eyes glinting like steel. "So that leaves us with one last bit of business."

"What?" I asked. "We need to get this to Abhi."

"Humans may not partake of the Fountain, nor use it to heal a mortal," said Mr. O formally.

"Why not? We've paid the price. And besides, my dog Fib's been healing people all summer," said Ben.

Mr. O addressed Ben. "He is a beast, and pure of heart. The Fountain is not meant for humans. You cannot take the water. You cannot use it to help your friend."

He reached out and took the bottle from Ben like he was a toddler.

"But we have to help Abhi," I said.

Mr. O shook his head. "I'm afraid you cannot." He tilted his head and considered me. "Unless . . ."

"Unless what?" I asked.

"Unless you agree to take the blame for the vomiting incident at your championship game."

My stomach dropped to my toes. "But . . . but that's a lie."

Mr. O nodded. "Yes, but a very believable one. You delivered the snacks, did you not? If you admit to altering them, no one will blame the Salt Shaker. In fact, we will be seen as a dupe in your nefarious plot, and that should drive even more business our way." He smiled and cracked his knuckles.

"But . . . everyone will hate me. Not just in Bridgeton. In Comity, too." All summer long, I'd struggled to make friends. And now that I finally had some, and had found my place in this town, it would all go away. And then there was Mom. I could only imagine how horrified she'd be if she thought I'd poisoned opponents—physically hurt them on purpose—to try to win a baseball game.

"It's your choice, my dear. Your friend's health, or your reputation."

"Don't do it, Trish. We'll find another way," said Ben. "I'll say I poisoned the snacks. Everyone knows how obsessed I am with winning."

I shook my head. "No one will believe that. I always got the snacks from the Salt Shaker. And I'm the one who left them in the Camemberts' dugout."

"There is no other way," said Mr. O.

He was right.

"You've got to understand," said Rob. "There's a wager going on here. And our side needs to win."

Luna said nothing but watched me with her bright yellow eyes, and it unnerved me.

"You can't make Trish lie about something like this," Ben protested.

My mind raced. I squeezed Ben's hand. "It's okay," I said.

"It's not okay. It is the opposite of okay!" Ben said.

"I'll do it," I said. I let out my breath. "I'll do it to save Abhi. I'll say I poisoned the Camemberts' snacks."

Chapter Thirty-Four

Ben

Gifts and Consequences

"Trish," I said. "You can't do it. Abhi wouldn't want you to."

"Abhi doesn't get a choice. We need to heal him," Trish said. "I'll be fine."

Luna stared at Trish. She hadn't blinked in five minutes, and it was giving me the creeps.

"Trish—"

"I said I'd made my choice. Mr. O, can we have the bottle back, please? We need to get going."

Mr. O started toward us, but Luna's voice interrupted him. "You would let her do this? To win a wager?"

Trish and I looked at each other.

A bemused smile played on Mr. O's face. "Of course, Luna. You know how important the Midsummer's Wager is."

"You have no interest in the fact that your *dear* Robin did no work at the Salt Shaker this summer, that he's been off doing whatever he pleases, while the rest of us worked hard in your service?"

"Hey! I've been doing things," said Robin.

But Luna's gaze was fixed on Mr. O. She walked slowly toward him. "You have no interest in the fact that Robin took the Books of Power, the ones for *us* to use, and gave them to these young people? That these mortals used the books to create magic that caused havoc in this town, the one you claim to care so much about?"

"Uh, we don't want to interfere. Could we have the bottle, and we'll be on our way?" I asked. But no one was paying any attention to me.

Luna was getting closer and closer to Mr. O, and he was looking at her with wide eyes. Rob kept taking his sparkly hat off and putting it back on.

"And oh, my king, you have no interest in who's been sabotaging our store this summer? Who could it be? What minions of Queen Titania could have had access to our store? And your dear, dear Robin, so unaware. So unconcerned." She had come right up to Mr. O's face.

Something fluttered in the air in front of us. A lot of somethings, large and pale green, with eyes on their wings.

"You are not worthy of my service, oh great King of The Wild."

"Luna!" Rob cried.

Mr. O narrowed his eyes. "Is that right, Luna?"

"Don't worry, neither is the queen. Don't you want to know what I've been busy doing this summer?"

I tilted my head. Trish nodded, and we began inching toward Mr. O. We just needed to grab the bottle.

"What are you talking about, Luna?" Mr. O asked sharply.

"I think it's time you learned my full name, my king," Luna said slowly, her voice growing louder. The pale green moths swirled in a spiral around her head.

Mr. O took a step back. Trish and I took a step toward him. Whatever happened here, we needed that bottle.

"It is not just Luna. It's . . ."

The moths arrayed themselves behind her like two gigantic wings made out of wings.

"*Moth.*"

Wait. Wasn't that another character from the play? Trish and I shared a confused look.

Rob sprang in front of Mr. O to shield him. "I knew we shouldn't have trusted you. You are sworn to the queen!"

Luna's eyes flashed. "I am sworn to no one. I have been sabotaging the Salt Shaker's snacks, to see if anyone would notice. But other than the mortals, no one did." She laughed harshly. "And even the mortals were too focused on winning to care. You speak of cooperation between Robin and myself,

King Oberon. But you and your wife are embroiled in an endless rivalry. How can you teach a lesson you yourself have not learned?"

"How dare you, spirit?" Mr. O thundered.

"Oh, I dare much more than this, oh mighty king," Luna sneered.

We were within feet of Mr. O. If we could just get our hands on that bottle . . .

"I now have two Books of Power. I'm going to keep them. And perhaps I'll give them to someone else, someone who truly understands what cooperation is. Phi, indeed, oh king. You have no idea what that means."

"I forbid it," said Mr. O, and his voice shivered through the air like a cold wind.

"Too late," said Luna with a smile. She turned to Trish and me. "Good luck, kids," she said.

The moths surrounded us like a green cloud.

When they finally flew away, we were back in my yard.

Chapter Thirty-Five

Trish

Forgiveness

"We have to go back!" Ben cried. We were back in his yard, blinking in the sudden sunlight.

"Let's go," I said.

Stopping only to grab another water bottle, we ran back through the woods. But this time, we had no map, and no Fib, and it took us much longer to find the two evergreens leaning upon each other. We crouched and went through.

And we found ourselves on another part of the path. There was no hill, no path leading to the Fountain.

"What's going on? This is just the normal Comity Woods," Ben said.

I touched his arm. "I don't think we can get through now, Ben. Not without Fib."

"Fib!" Ben called. "Fib, where are you?"

But there was no answer.

Eventually, we had to give up. "Fib will come back, Ben." But our hopes of bringing back something magical to save Abhi had disappeared with the fairies. Even if I publicly confessed to poisoning the Camemberts, would the fairies return with the water from the Fountain of Youth?

Every step seemed to take a month. We finally got across Ben's yard and into the house.

"You're back. Finally," said Claudia. "We've been trying to reach you. Abhi's home."

Abhi's mom opened the door flanked by the twins. "Oh, Ben. Oh, Trish," she said. "Abhi will be so happy to see you. Come in, please."

She hugged Ben, and then to my surprise, she turned and wrapped her arms around me. "Bless you, Trisha," she whispered. "If your mother wasn't at that game, I don't know what would have happened."

I didn't know what to say. If I hadn't been on the team, maybe Abhi wouldn't have been hurt in the first place? But she was right. Things would have been much worse if Mom hadn't been there.

We pulled apart, and Abhi's mom wiped her eyes. "Go and see him," she said.

"Hi, Ben. Hi, Trish," said the twins. Their pent-up energy was gone.

"Hey, Asha, Aadya. How's it going?" Ben asked.

"Okay," said Asha.

"Abhi's expecting you," said Aadya.

Ben and I followed the twins upstairs and hovered at the door to Abhi's room. I suddenly felt awkward. Did Abhi remember anything about the game? What if he was angry? And was there any chance he'd believe our explanation for what had happened?

"Don't worry," said Aadya.

"What?" I asked, startled.

"He's excited to see you," Asha said. "He's still the same person."

The twins clearly still knew everything I was thinking.

We knocked on Abhi's door.

"Come in," came Abhi's voice.

Ben nodded at me, and we steeled ourselves and went into the room.

Abhi's dad was sitting at his bed and stood as soon as we came in. "Thank you for coming," he said. "Abhi's been telling me all about your adventures on the baseball team."

Ben and I gave each other a nervous glance. "Really?" Ben asked.

"Just the most important parts," said Abhi. He was in

pajamas and propped up on pillows in his bed. His face was tired.

"I'll give you some privacy," Abhi's dad said. "Abhi, I'll be back later. Call if you need anything." He crossed the room and closed the door behind him.

"Okay," said Abhi. "Tell me all about what's been going on."

"Well," Ben said. "It's been quite a couple of days. But first, I have to say I'm sorry."

At Abhi's look of confusion, Ben launched into his confession about us not solving the math problem so he couldn't magic the ball away from Abhi during the game. "Can you forgive me?" he asked.

Abhi raised his eyebrows. "Dude, there's nothing to forgive. That Bridgeton kid has power, and who knows whether you'd have been able to change the course of that ball."

"But—"

"And I should have been able to get my glove up, or step out of the way, or duck, or something. But I was distracted."

I thought I'd seen Abhi turn his head right as the ball was hit. "By what?"

"Right after I threw that pitch, I looked up and saw my dad. He finally made it to one of my games. That's why I didn't see the ball coming back."

"Oh, man, Abhi." Ben ran his hand over his face.

"How's he taking it?" I asked.

Abhi shrugged. "He was pretty broken up about it. Said he should have been at every single game, that he was so sorry he'd given me such a hard time about everything, and that he didn't know what he'd do if he'd lost me."

"What did you say to him?" Ben asked.

Abhi's smile lit up his face. "I told him not to blame himself. I knew he was just trying to be a good dad to me, and, like Trish's mom said, there was a one in a million chance that this would happen. I told him he didn't need my forgiveness, but I forgave him anyway."

Something melted in my chest, and my breathing came easier than it had for days. Abhi was right. *Forgiveness.* All summer long I'd been holding on to anger at Mom about dragging me to another new home. And Abhi nearly died, but he forgave his dad in a second without him even needing to ask. Abhi understood things that were way more important than math puzzles or winning baseball games.

"Now tell me what you've been doing. Did you ever solve that final puzzle?" Abhi leaned back against his pillow. "I want to hear everything."

Chapter Thirty-Six

Ben

Confessions

We told Abhi everything that had happened: the final math puzzle, the ultimate answer, and our adventure in the woods. We told him about the fairies and the Fountain of Youth, the moths, and Fib.

"Wow," he said.

"Hard to believe, isn't it?" I said. "But it's all true. We didn't leave anything out, right, Trish?"

Trish nodded. "We told you everything, Abhi. I'm so sorry we couldn't bring any of that magical water back for you."

Abhi furrowed his brow. "I couldn't let you lie about cheating at the game."

Trish shrugged. "It wouldn't have been that bad."

Abhi raised his eyebrows. "It would have been awful. But thanks for being willing to do it."

"How are you feeling?" I asked. "And what did the doctors say?"

Abhi turned away.

"You don't have to answer if you don't want to," Trish said quickly.

"I was just thinking, that's all," Abhi said. "You know, Trish, your mom is amazing. In addition to saving my life, she helped keep my parents sane while I was in the hospital."

"I know," Trish said. "I've been mad at her for so long that I kind of forgot what a great doctor she is, and how important she is to her patients and their families."

"And your dad, Ben," Abhi said to me. "He got better at coaching, huh? Better at listening, that's for sure."

My face heated up. "Dude, you knew it. You always said I should give him another chance to be head coach."

"The docs say I've got a bruise on my heart." Abhi rubbed his chest gently. "Based on the one I've got on the outside, I can only imagine how ugly the one on the inside is." He opened his shirt and showed us a horrible purple bruise. He started to laugh, but then stopped and put his hand on his chest. "Anyway, my heart isn't squeezing normally yet. I'm okay lying in bed, but I get tired easily. Like, I can't walk more than a hallway or talk too long without becoming exhausted. The doctors say we just have to wait and see how much my heart recovers. They ran like a million tests, and there wasn't much else for them to do for me in the hospital, so they let me come home."

Not able to walk more than a hallway! "Will you . . . will you be able to play sports again?" I asked.

"I don't know," Abhi said. "If I can't run, I don't think I can play. But you never know."

I hung my head. "If you don't play, I'm not sure I want to."

Trish looked between Abhi and me. "Me neither."

Abhi laughed, and then stopped and clutched his chest again. "You two are something else. I'm glad I gave you both that shove this summer."

"What does that mean?" Trish asked.

Abhi looked back and forth at us sheepishly. "I have a confession to make. Remember when I told you that Ben wanted to be friends with you?"

"Yeah?" Trish said.

Uh-oh. I had a feeling I knew where this was going. "You didn't."

Abhi nodded.

I turned to Trish. "He said the same thing to me! It wasn't true?"

Abhi shrugged. "Not technically true, not at that time. Neither of you had actually told me that you wanted to be friends with the other. But I knew that deep down, you both did."

"Dude!" I said.

"Abhi!" Trish said at the same time.

Abhi spread his hands. "Clearly it worked out. Phi, not primes, remember? *Come, come, we are friends.*"

And we were.

There was a scratching at the door, and I opened it. Fib stood in the doorway with his coat gleaming, his eyes shining, something held in his green-dusted mouth. "There you are, boy," I said. "You found your way back."

Fib trotted into the room, his nails clicking on the floor, and dropped what he'd brought into my hand. Then he went straight to Abhi's bed and leaped up.

"Hi there, Fib," said Abhi. "It's good to see you."

Fib climbed into Abhi's lap and nestled his head on Abhi's chest. Abhi winced for a split second, then leaned back against the pillow and yawned. "I'm feeling tired all of a sudden," he said.

"Ben . . ." Trish pointed at the green dust on Fib's muzzle, his paws, his belly. Fib was covering Abhi in that dust. He was putting it right on Abhi's chest, right over his heart.

"Go ahead and sleep, dude. We'll be right here," I said.

And Trish and I stayed that way, watching the rise and fall of Abhi's chest, the spiral on Fib's forehead gleaming in the afternoon sunlight.

By the time Abhi's dad came upstairs a little later, we

thought Abhi's breathing had eased. And when Fib hopped down from the bed, he did it slowly, like the old dog he was. He limped to my side, and when he gazed up at me, his muzzle was gray again.

It turned out that magic did have a cost, after all.

I looked at what Fib had brought me. It was a baseball. Dad's ball, covered in blue writing. I traced my signature with my thumb. And tied around it was Trish's bracelet, the one that she'd made for me weeks ago. I slipped it off the ball and onto my wrist.

"Come on, Fib," I said. "Let's go home."

When I got home I found Dad in the living room watching the Turkeys. They were leading 4–2 against the Red Apples. I sat next to him on the sofa.

"How's Abhi doing?" he asked.

"Pretty well," I said. "I have a feeling he's going to make a full recovery."

"Thank goodness," said Dad. "What an unbelievable week it's been."

"I wanted to tell you something," I said, still watching the TV. "You were great during the championship game. And I'm going to sign up for fall ball, in case you're interested in coaching."

Dad's eyes widened. "Really, Ben? I loved being an assistant coach this summer. You played your heart out all season, but especially in that last game, the strangest game I've ever witnessed. I'm so proud of you—the whole team, of course, but especially you. You've became quite a leader."

"I loved playing ball again. At first I wasn't so sure I wanted to, because it reminded me of Grandma. But you were right. She would have wanted me to play ball again. Especially with you. I'm sorry it took me so long to figure that out." I turned back to the game again. The Turkeys needed just three more outs.

Dad's voice was soft and low. "After Grandma died, I blamed myself for a long time. I know you blamed me, too."

He knew? I thought I was keeping my anger secret. One of the Red Apples hit a pop-up to the shortstop. One out.

"But I want you to know. About Grandma, and about Abhi," Dad said. "I want you to know that it's not your fault. None of it. Not what happened to Abhi, or what happened two years ago to Grandma." His voice broke, and there were tears in Dad's eyes.

"Dad—"

"Just let me finish. Goodness knows I've blamed myself. But sometimes bad things happen to good people, Ben, and it's no one's fault. All we can do is go on living. I've been pressuring you to play ball when I know how painful it's been for you. I'm sorry. Can you forgive me?"

What had Abhi said? "You were just doing your best," I said. "There's nothing to forgive. But I forgive you anyway."

"I love you so much, Ben."

"Love you, too, Dad."

And we hugged in a way that we hadn't since Grandma died.

I glanced at the screen. There was a runner on first. The batter hit into a double play. The game was over, and the Turkeys had won.

"There's just one thing I need you to do," I said.

"Anything," said Dad.

"Get that chest thing checked out, okay? The one that's giving you trouble almost every day?"

Dad looked at me for a second, then smiled and said, "Deal."

I pulled the ball out of my pocket. The evening sun was low in a cloudless sky. It was the perfect summer day. A perfect day for baseball.

"Hey Dad," I said. "Want to have a catch?"

Chapter Thirty-Seven

Trish

The Picnic

I was sitting at the computer in the kitchen waiting for Mom when she came home.

"How did it go?" I asked.

She seemed tired but relieved. "Another open artery," said Mom. "Another good night. Sorry I'm home so late."

I tucked my hair behind my ear. "That's okay. I'm proud of you, Mom."

"I'm proud of you, too, Trisha. I know it hasn't been easy for you, moving again." Mom dropped her bag and kissed me on the forehead. "I know you've been angry, with good reason. I haven't been here for you since we moved. I've been too busy taking care of everyone else, when I should have put more effort into taking care of you."

"It's okay," I said. "I know what you're doing is important. If you hadn't been at the game, Abhi might not be alive."

"I'm glad I was there. But there are other people who can use an AED. There aren't any others who can be your mom. I should have found a way to be there for every game. I'm sorry."

"I've been angry at you for so long, but you're just doing what you love, in the best way you can. Just like me. And I have to tell you something," I said.

Mom pulled a chair next to me and sat. "What is it?"

And I told her about the Math Puzzler competition, the mistaken scoring, and how I hadn't been able to tell anyone. Mom listened.

She put a hand on my cheek. "Oh, Trish, you've been keeping that secret for a while, huh?"

I nodded. "It was awful. I know how proud you were of my getting first place, and didn't want to disappoint you."

"Why would I blame you for the judges' mistake? Although I wish you'd felt you could tell me sooner. And Ben needs to know."

"I already told him," I said. "A couple of weeks ago."

"Good," said Mom. "And given how much time you've been spending together, I take it this means he's not upset with you, either?"

"He was amazingly chill about the whole thing," I said. "Even before Abhi got hurt and we realized that all this competition is supposed to bring us together, not split us apart."

"I'm glad," said Mom. "And we should contact the Puzzler judges, to see if he can get a medal, too. After all, you tied."

I grinned. "He'd like that."

"Aren't you tired? We should both go to bed," said Mom.

"There's one more thing I need your help with," I said.

"Anything."

"Can you help me sign up for fall ball?"

Mom raised her eyebrows. "I'm surprised you didn't ask Dad. He was your coach this summer, after all."

"I wanted you to know. I wanted to make sure you agreed."

"It's your decision, Trish," Mom said. "I would never tell you not to do what you love."

I nodded. "I wanted you to know that I'm signing up because of you."

"What does that mean?"

"It might be hard for me to compete on the big field. But I'm going to try. Just like you do, every day. In the hospital, in your lab. And in our home."

Mom's cheeks flushed, and she touched my hair gently. "You know, I've gotten used to this look on you," she said. "I like it." She kissed the top of my head. "Now tell me what you need me to do."

We filled out the online registration form and put in the payment.

And that was that.

"Are you coming to the baseball picnic in a couple of weeks?" I asked.

"Wouldn't miss it for the world," said Mom.

It was still warm, but I could feel a hint of fall's crispness in the air. September was around the corner, and school would start soon. Brad waved at me from his unicycle as I crossed the parking lot and stepped into Bailey Park. Sanjay and Claudia strolled by holding hands. Fib snoozed under a tree, moving his paws in a doggy dream.

I couldn't stop grinning when I found Abhi and Ben. "Just another couple of weeks," I said.

"I know," said Abhi. "We are going to have so much fun this fall!"

I nodded. "It will be different."

"It'll be different for *all* of us," Ben said. "And we'll be in it together."

"Here," I said. "I made one for each of us. Hold out your wrists."

They did, and I tied bracelets on them. Green, blue, and white. Salt Shaker colors. The day after Abhi came home from the hospital, a letter from the Salt Shaker had appeared in the *Comity Journal* saying that an ingredient they'd added to the Camemberts' snacks had gone bad and made everyone sick, and they were shutting down the store. No one was going to miss those Sports Crisps or the weird side effects they caused. But I would miss our summer team.

"How're you feeling?" I asked Abhi.

"Never better. The docs say my heart is back to normal."

"My man," said Ben, bumping his fist. "And my dad got checked out, too, and his heart is fine. All that chest pain was actually his stomach."

"Speaking of dads, take a look," Abhi said, pointing to the baseball field.

To my surprise, I realized Dad and Coach Joe were tossing to a third man: Abhi's dad.

"Since when did your dad start playing ball?" Ben asked.

"Since we all got to meet the Turkeys," Abhi said with a laugh. "I'm glad the Camemberts got to come, too. I guess they aren't so terrible, once you get to know them."

"They ended up being okay," said Ben. "And when they annoy me I just think of the beautiful memory of them barfing all over the field."

We all laughed, and then Abhi's face grew serious. "After I recovered, I figured Dad had even more reasons for me not to play ball. But he said my getting hurt finally made him realize that he should be proud of the person I am, and not the person he wanted me to be. I'm going to audition for the fall play. Oh and speaking of signing up for things,

I've decided on something else." His cheeks turned red.

"Don't tell me you're switching to lacrosse," Ben said.

"No way," Abhi said with a snort.

"Well then what is it?" I asked.

Abhi kicked at the dirt. "Well, given that I've been hanging around you guys . . ." He paused.

"What? Spill it, dude," Ben said.

"I'm trying out for the Math Puzzler team."

Ben and I glanced at each other, then back at Abhi.

"You're kidding," Ben said.

Abhi furrowed his brow. "Dumb idea?"

"Awesome idea," I said. "You'll be so fantastic! We can work on problems together to prepare."

"Don't leave me out," Ben said. "There's a lot I could learn from you, dude."

Abhi's grin lit up his whole face. He held out his hand, and the bracelet stood out against his skin. "Phi for the win."

I put my hand on Abhi's, and Ben put his on mine. "Phi, not primes," we said in unison.

"*We'll have dancing afterward*," said Abhi.

Ben looked horrified. "That had better be a Shakespeare quote, and not an actual desire to dance."

We cracked up.

"Let's get something to eat," Abhi said.

"I could go for some potato chips," Ben said.

"How about some Sports Crisps?" I asked.

"Definitely not," said Abhi, laughing.

With the way the summer had started, who could have calculated that this would have happened? Somehow, this ratio was just right. Everyone was getting their share of the sun. Baseball was magic. Math was magic, too. And thanks to them both, I had family and friends, in the perfect proportion.

Acknowledgments

Many authors will tell you that second books are hard—and this book is no exception. Although *Much Ado About Baseball* is my third novel to be published, it was the second novel I'd written, and it wasn't always easy to write. I knew I wanted to tell this story about "Team Oberon" from the *Midsummer's Mayhem* world during the same strange summer in the town of Comity. Figuring out the motivations of the characters and writing a dual point of view book was challenging at times, but I did it with the help of many friends. If the journey of *Midsummer's Mayhem* was about believing I could write a book and have it published, the journey of *Much Ado About Baseball* was about finding my people.

I could not have written this book without my amazing critique partners—especially Theresa Milstein, who invited me to join her critique group and helped me find the way forward when I was really and truly stuck. Many thanks to Donna Woelki, Lisa Rogers, Victoria Coe, Judy Mintz, and Jaya Mehta. Alison Goldberg, Sharon Abra Hanen, Shannon Falkson, Casey Breton, and Chelsea Dill saw many, many versions of these chapters, and to them, I'm forever grateful.

Brent Taylor, my brilliant agent, encouraged me and told me he had every confidence in my ability to write this book. As usual, he was right.

It's been such a pleasure to work on a second novel with my wonderful editor, Charlie Ilgunas. I so appreciate his love of this book (and of baseball and math!) and all his help in getting to the heart of this story. Many thanks to the whole team at Yellow Jacket/Little Bee Books, including Ryan Jenkins, copyeditor; Dave Barrett, managing editor; and extraordinary publicist Paul Crichton. Designer Natalie Padberg Bartoo, and artist Chloe Dijon created the perfect cover and interior illustrations that made Trish, Ben, and the other characters come to life.

When I was a kid, I loved reading books about smart kids solving puzzles, so it's no surprise that I now write these kinds of stories. My husband and I have had so much fun over the years sharing puzzles and riddles with our kids; there was always a competition to see who got the logic puzzle book during plane rides! This story was inspired by my math-loving, baseball-playing son and husband, but also by my bold and brilliant daughter who strives for excellence in the classroom and on the field. My family is the Fountain of Joy from which all my creativity flows, and I can never thank them enough.

Baked Sports Crisps

Serves 4

Ingredients

2 medium-sized potatoes (russet or Yukon Gold)
1 ½ tablespoons olive oil
¾ teaspoon salt
Pepper to taste
Spices: I like a combination of paprika, garlic powder, onion powder, and cayenne pepper, but you can use anything you like.
Fresh herbs (optional): You can finely chop parsley, cilantro, or chives to add some freshness.

Directions

1. Preheat the oven to 400°F. Cover a baking sheet with parchment paper.
2. Scrub and completely dry the potatoes. Using a sharp knife or mandoline, thinly slice the potatoes (1⁄16" is best, but it can be up to ⅛"). Pat the potato slices dry with a clean kitchen towel.
3. Toss the potato slices with olive oil, salt, and pepper. I also add ½ tsp garlic powder, 1 tsp paprika, ¼ tsp onion powder, and ⅛ tsp cayenne pepper.
4. Place on the prepared pan in a single layer, not too close together.
5. Bake for 15-18 minutes, flipping halfway through, until crispy. Watch carefully to make sure they don't burn.
6. Allow to cool briefly, toss with fresh herbs (if using), then enjoy!

Yummy Onion Dip

Serves 8

Ingredients

1 ½ cups sour cream
⅛ cup mayonnaise
1 tablespoon minced, dried onion
1 ½ teaspoon onion powder
¼ teaspoon garlic powder
¼ teaspoon salt
a pinch black pepper
1 tablespoon finely chopped fresh chives

Directions

1. Mix together sour cream and mayonnaise.
2. Stir in minced dried onion, onion powder, garlic powder, salt, and pepper.
3. Sprinkle with finely chopped fresh chives, dip your chips, and enjoy!

Mathematical Concepts and Puzzles

As Ben notes in the story, baseball is indeed full of numbers and statistics! Here are some common ones that people often cite to gauge how a player is doing.

- Hitting Statistics: the higher the better
- Batting Average is the number of hits a player gets divided by the number of at-bats: AVG = hits / at-bats
- Slugging Percentage is singles plus doubles (x 2) plus triples (x 3) plus home runs (x 4), all divided by the number of at-bats: SLG = 1B + 2B(2) + 3B(3) + HR(4) / at-bats
- Pitching Statistics: the lower the better
- Earned Run Average is the number of earned runs (runs not due to errors) divided by innings pitched, multiplied by 9: ERA = (Earned Runs/Innings Pitched) x 9
- Walks + Hits Per Innings Pitched is walks plus hits divided by the number of innings pitched: WHIP = Walks + Hits / Innings Pitched

Fibonacci, the Fibonacci Sequence, and the Golden Ratio

As Ben and Trish explain in the story, Leonardo Bonacci, whose nickname was Fibonacci, was a thirteenth-century Italian mathematician. He traveled the world as part of his family's trading business and learned about mathematics from other cultures, including those in India and the Middle East. In 1202, he wrote a book on mathematics called *Liber Abaci*, in which he popularized the Hindu-Arabic number system—using the digits 0 through 9—as a more efficient way to do mathematics as compared with Roman numerals. In the book, he described what we now call the Fibonacci sequence of numbers, in which each subsequent number is the sum of the two before it: 0, 1, 1, 2, 3, 5, 8, 13, 21, 34, 55, 89, and so on.

These numbers are often found in nature, such as in trees, flowers, fruits, and vegetables. As the numbers get larger, the ratio between them gets closer and closer to phi, or the "golden ratio," which is an irrational number (never ending, never repeating) that is close to 1.618. This ratio is also found over and over in nature, from seashells to hurricanes, and even in the human body. For example, the ratio of the length of the whole arm to the lower part of the arm. This ratio is also used in art and architecture to create aesthetically pleasing work.

Divisibility Tricks

When solving math puzzles, it's sometimes useful to quickly see if something is divisible by another number.

- It's easy to tell if something is divisible by 2: If it's an even number, it's divisible by 2!

But what about other numbers? Here are some quick and easy tricks.

- A number is divisible by 3 if the *sum of its digits* is divisible by 3! So, 211,140 is divisible by 3, because 2 + 1 + 1 + 1 + 4 + 0 = 9, which is divisible by 3.
- A number is divisible by 4 if its *last 2 digits* are divisible by 4! So, we know that 8,477,424 is divisible by 4 because 24 is divisible by 4.
- A number is divisible by 5 if *it ends in 0 or 5*. (You probably already knew this!)
- A number is divisible by 6 if *it's divisible by both 2 and 3*! So, it needs to end in an even number *and* the sum of its digits need to be divisible by 3! For example, 204 ends in an even number and 2 + 4 = 6 which is divisible by 3, so the whole number is divisible by 6.
- To see if a number is divisible by 7, take that last digit "off" and double it. Then subtract that answer from the rest of the digits like they are a new number. If that answer is divisible by 7, then the whole number is! If the new number

is also large, you can keep doing this trick until it's easy to tell. For example, look at 5,327. Take 7 x 2 = 14. 532 - 14 is 518. I don't know whether 518 is divisible by 7. So, I can take 8 x 2 = 16. 51 –16 = 35, which *is* divisible by 7, so the whole number is divisible by 7!

- A number is divisible by 8 if its *last 3 digits* are divisible by 8. For example, look at 516,240. Since 240 is divisible by 8, the whole number is divisible by 8.
- A number is divisible by 9 if *the sum of its digits* is divisible by 9! Take a look at 999,108. The sum of the digits is 9 + 9 + 9 + 1 + 0 + 8 = 36, which is divisible by 9, so the whole number is divisible by 9.
- A number is divisible by 10 *if it ends in 0*. (You probably already knew this!)
- To see if a number is divisible by 11, add the odd digits and the even digits separately. Subtract one from the other. If the answer is divisible by 11, the whole number is. For example, look at the number 3729. 3 + 2 = 5 and 7 + 9 = 16. 16 – 5 = 11, which is divisible by 11, so the whole number is.
- A number is divisible by 12 if *it's divisible by both 3 and 4*! So, its digit sum should be divisible by 3 and its last two digits should be divisible by 4! Let's look at 6,852: 6 + 8 + 5 + 2 = 21 which is divisible by 3. And 52 is divisible by 4. So, 6,852 is divisible by 12.

SUDOKU

Sudoku is a type of puzzle that involves placing objects (usually numbers) on a grid so that no number is repeated in a row, column, or "block." In the book, Ben and Trish have to solve this type of puzzle using six letters, but more traditional sudoku usually involve numbers in a 9 x 9 grid. Here's one for you to solve:

6		9	8	1			3	5
8			7			2		
	3			2				4
			9		7		4	8
9		5				6		7
3	7		4		2			
4				8			7	
		3			9			6
2	1			4	5	9		3

Solution

6	2	9	8	1	4	7	3	5
8	5	4	7	9	3	2	6	1
7	3	1	5	2	6	8	9	4
1	6	2	9	5	7	3	4	8
9	4	5	1	3	8	6	2	7
3	7	8	4	6	2	1	5	9
4	9	6	3	8	1	5	7	2
5	8	3	2	7	9	4	1	6
2	1	7	6	4	5	9	8	3

A Couple of Poem Riddles

The more of it there is,
the less you see.
What is it?

Answer: Darkness

When I'm flesh and I'm blood,
in the darkness, I roam.
When I'm metal or wood,
I help you get home.
What am I?

Answer: A bat